Dreamland
The Journey Begins

Dreamland

The Journey Begins

Cheryl Rodd

Copyright © 2023 by Cheryl Rodd.

All rights reserved. No part of this book may be reproduced in any form or by any electronic or mechanical means, including information storage and retrieval systems, without permission in writing from the author and publisher, except by reviewers, who may quote brief passages in a review.

ISBN: 978-1-961096-54-7   (Paperback Edition)
ISBN: 978-1-961096-55-4   (Hardcover Edition)
ISBN: 978-1-961096-53-0   (E-book Edition)

Some characters and events in this book are fictitious. Any similarity to the real persons, living or dead, is coincidental and not intended by the author.

Book Ordering Information

The Regency Publishers, US
521 5th Ave 17th floor NY, NY10175
Phone Number: (315)537-3088 ext 1007
Email: info@theregencypublishers.com
www.theregencypublishers.com

Printed in the United States of America

Contents

Summary iii

Chapter 1 1

Chapter 2 5

Chapter 3 11

Chapter 4 20

Chapter 5 25

Chapter 6 31

Chapter 7 36

Chapter 8 41

Chapter 9 47

Chapter 10 51

Chapter 11 54

Chapter 12 59

Chapter 13 64

Chapter 14 70

Chapter 15 76

Chapter 16 87

Chapter 17 95

Chapter 18 101

Chapter 19 107

Chapter 20 112

Chapter 21 120

Chapter 22 125

Chapter 23 132

Chapter 24 138

Chapter 25 143

Chapter 26 150

Chapter 27 156

Chapter 28 161

Chapter 29 166

SUMMARY

Dreamland is a parallel universe with as many facets as are in the conscious world. Everyone who sleeps has gone there. Some remember and some don't.

Everyone thinks it is all in our subconscious mind and that our imagination has created it, but Dreamland is there all the time, we are the transient visitors. Our state of mind, our level of relaxation and our hopes and fears just determine what area of Dreamland we visit each Night.

Sometimes, we have to face our fears or enemies and other times we are in a certain area of Dreamland to learn important things about ourselves, our past or our future.

Dreamland is as real a place as where we live in our waking hours. There are permanent residents there, both good and evil. They have a Dream Keeper in charge of the entire place and Division Masters for each area. The guides that lead us through our visits are sometimes unseen to us, but they are always with us. They are either Dream Gnomes or Nightmare Fairies. Everything we can imagine, good and evil, is all there. There are beautiful forests, fields, oceans, sunsets, human emotion, and ominous swamps with crawling, slithering creatures throughout.

Now we know that it is always there. What would happen if the fabric that separates us from Dreamland did tear, even slightly, what then?

Chapter 1

It started like any other dream Tara ever had. Floating, happily, as a 7-year-old does, between her own world and Dreamland. She was dressed in a flowing angelic white gown as she flew and floated through the darkened streets of her own neighborhood.

As she floated happily, over the familiar rooftops of her friends' homes, she noticed a sudden damp chill in the air. It was like a misty, cold wave of fear and darkness.

Suddenly, she was standing in an old-fashioned parlor, in front of a huge set of glass doors. They were like French doors with the wood slats all through them and gold trim around each individual pane of glass. As Tara turned from the window, slowly, as in a dream, she saw the outline of a small child curled up, in a huge, overstuffed chair in front of an ornate fireplace. The fire seemed to be slowly dying out as the red and yellow flames slowly danced in a row over a tiny pile of glowing embers. The child, crying as if his heart was breaking, seemed not to know Tara was even there.

Tara edged closer to the sobbing child. As she neared the chair the boy bolted upright, from his fetal position, at the sound of her footsteps. When their eyes met, he bolted from the chair into Tara's outstretched arms. Tara was so surprised that her arms had even been outstretched, let alone that he had jumped into them, that she lost her balance and fell backwards. Just as she felt herself fall, she glanced over her shoulder, and much to her relief, she noticed another overstuffed chair there to break their fall. They landed with a thud and the little boy on top of her giggled. His wide eyes and shy smile made her giggle too.

"Mama, mama your back!" he shrieked.

Tara looked down at herself and realized that she was not 7 years old anymore. She was a grown woman, obviously a mother, and dressed in early 19th century clothing, complete with lace up boots. Before she could fully digest this amazing and spontaneous transition, she could hear herself speaking.

"There, there now Seth. What is all this fuss about? I was only in the kitchen making our hot cocoa." Tara soothed.

Tara's mind was reeling. How could she be this little boy's mother when she was only a 7-year-old girl a minute ago? The only explanation she could find was that she was in Dreamland and that this little boy must need her there for a reason. So, she decided to relax and just see where all this would lead them as the dream unfolded.

No sooner had Tara made this decision when she and Seth heard an incredible crash. It sounded like it was directly over the house. Seth clung to her even harder now and began whimpering. Tara knew that their only hope was to follow her "gut" instincts, because she had no idea what to expect. This dream drama was about Seth not Tara the 7 year old. She had to become his mother in order to really help him. Suddenly, another loud bang. This time it felt like it was inside the house, upstairs. Sheer terror overtook her senses as she grabbed Seth's little hand and slowly rose from their chair.

"The shelter." she heard herself whisper to Seth.

"Yippee!" Seth exclaimed.

The words were barely out of his mouth when they were on foot hurrying toward the parlor door to the hall. Seth was leading the way and Tara could only assume they were headed for the shelter that she, herself had mentioned. Seth dragged her through the enormous kitchen at the back of the house then, down a long hallway, through another narrow door, left, and then down a winding hallway. Seth stopped short in front of a small door that looked to Tara to be too small to even fit through.

"The key, Mama, the key!" Seth whispered urgently.

Tara searched through the folds of her antique housedress until she finally found a hidden pocket, just behind her waistband. She gently pulled on a ribbon that was pinned to the pocket lining. When she pulled, she could feel something sliding out of the pocket. It was an ancient skeleton key tied to the ribbon. She immediately grabbed it and slid it into the keyhole of this odd door. Much to her surprise the key not only fit, but it also turned and the door swung open with such force that she and Seth were nearly knocked to the floor.

Tara gently shoved Seth behind the folds of her skirt as she peered carefully around the corner of the doorway. What she saw amazed her. The staircase was unlike anything she had ever seen. It was a spiral, but it was made of black iron. It looked like it wound around itself as it gradually led downwards. She clutched Seth's hand, and as they began their descent the stairway began to sway gently, back and forth. As Tara looked towards the ceiling, she could barely make out suspension cables of some kind. They creaked ominously as she and Seth stepped from one stair to the next. It was like walking on air. Seth clung to her skirt and hand as they slowly navigated each stair.

Tara was grateful for the kerosene lamp she had taken off the wall outside the doorway because there was no other light source on the stairs. It felt, to Tara, like they were entering the very core of the earth. The smell of dampness was almost overpowering.

There seemed to be no end to the staircase.

They slowly moved further down into the vast darkness with only the small lamp to guide them.

Suddenly there was a huge flash of light. It was a bright red color and it blinded Tara. She stumbled and felt herself falling for what seemed like an eternity. As she fell all she could hear was Seth's tiny, frightened voice screaming, "Mama, Mama, don't leave me here all alone. Mama, please…"

Mama, Mama, don't leave me here all alone. Mama, please…"

Chapter 2

Tara awoke bathed in sweat and screaming; "Mama, Mama don't leave me here all alone."

Katherine, hearing her daughters' distress, bolted up the stairs, two at a time. When she reached Tara's bedroom door, it was locked from the inside and there was an eerie red glow all around it.

"Tara, open this door, now!" Katherine screamed through the door.

"I can't Mommy. It's too hot." Tara whined back at her mother.

"Andrew come here, quickly, it's happening again!" Katherine bellowed to her husband.

"Kay, my Lord, you'll wake the dead screaming like that. What is it now?" Andrew shot back as he, too took the stairs two at a time.

Andrew reached the top step just in time to see the red glow fading. Tara's door flew open as if it had a mind of it's own and crashed against the wall.

"Dear God in Heaven, what now? " he muttered to himself.

Kay was on the bed, in one bound, holding her quaking daughter.

"It's okay, honey. It was only a dream. Everything is going to be all right. Mommy's here now honey." Kay crooned to her terrified child.

Andrew slowly approached and sat gently on the edge of the bed. He laid his hand on Kay's shoulder to soothe her, but the look of agony in her eyes was finally more than he could take.

"Honey, we need help. This can't go on any longer. This is not normal.," he whispered to his wife.

"Alright Drew, I'll go call Dr. Cain again and see if he has any new ideas for us. But I had better wait until morning, it's 3AM now." Kay relented.

"Tara, honey, you get some sleep now. Mommy will call Dr. Cain in the morning. Everything will be okay, just rest now." Kay whispered in a desperate attempt to comfort her child.

"No!" Tara shrieked. " I have to save Seth! The little boy. My little boy! I can't just leave him there all alone!" Tara was almost hysterical.

Kay nodded to Drew and he slowly backed out of the room, silently, He went to the upstairs den to call Dr. Cain. Lately, the dreams were more frequent, more graphic and Tara seemed to remember them better. After all, Dr. Cain was the best in his field, whatever his field was called. Dream phobia is what Drew was calling it lately.

The phone rang six times before a sleepy voice croaked, "Dr. Cain!"

It took Dr, Cain all of twenty minutes to get to the Prescott's house, which was actually a forty-minute ride. Kay already had the coffee on. Drew sat at the kitchen table, head in hands, trying to make some sense of this nightmare their life had become.

Tara had been having dreams as long as he could remember, but since she turned seven the dreams had become more frequent. They all seemed to have some hidden message in them. Like someone or something was trying to tell them something, important. Was Tara losing her mind?

Was the whole family in some kind of danger? All these months of therapy, hypnosis and dream analysis and still no closer to an answer and no real proof of anything at all.

Kay and Dr. Cain had been up in Tara's room for well over an hour, when they finally materialized in the kitchen doorway. Kay looked totally drained, and Dr. Cain looked perplexed and bewildered.

Kay poured them each a cup of coffee and refilled Drew's cup. When she finally sat down, she immediately put her head in her hands, elbows on the table and wept. She was feeling the effects of constant worry over her daughter's worsening condition, whatever condition that was? Not knowing what was wrong or how she could help her daughter was the worst part of all. Seeing her daughter distressed was taking its toll on both Andrew and Katherine.

Too weak and too exhausted to cry any longer, Kay raised her head from her hands and reached across the table to Drew's hand. As they sat together in silent misery, Dr. Cain was feverishly making notes.

"Okay folks." Dr. Cain finally announced, glancing from one to the other. "Here is what I propose," he continued hesitantly.

"The Sleep Centre has an opening and it is nearing the end of school for the summer. I think we should admit Tara immediately for some detailed clinical assessment." Dr. Cain paused and took a deep breath before continuing.

"The closeness between Kay and Tara is a strong soothing agent for both of you. That is why I believe that you, Kay should come with us." He raised his hand, open, to stave off any arguments and then continued.

"I know it will be difficult for you Drew, but the process will go more smoothly and a great deal faster if Kay and Tara are kept together." he sighed.

Okay, Doctor!" Drew began, "I love my wife and daughter more than anything. I know that they share a special bond. I also know that Tara would be much better off with Kay at her side. How long a process are we talking about, anyway?" Drew finally moved his gaze, although reluctantly, from Kay to Dr. Cain.

Dr. Cain drew in a long breath and looked from Kay to Drew and back again. "There is really no way to know for sure" he began. "It all depends on how quickly Tara responds to our sleep therapy program. With a little luck we could accomplish a great deal in a few short weeks."

The word "weeks" slammed into Drew like a hammer at top speed. He just gazed at Dr. Cain and whispered, "Will I be able to visit or at least call every day?"

"After the first week of orientation, initial testing and assessment, visits could be arranged." Dr Cain replied evenly.

"Well, I guess I could handle it for a week if it will help Tara at all. Tara cannot go on like this for much longer. She needs help, and if she can get it at the Sleep Centre, then I'm all for it." Drew finished, reluctantly.

"Kay, how do you feel about all this? You haven't even uttered a word since you sat down." Drew asked, with genuine concern in his voice.

"Well…" Kay began rather, shakily.

"I guess at this point we really have no other alternative. I'll get our things together tonight so we can leave first thing in the morning." she sighed.

Dr. Cain gave Kay a card with the Sleep Centre address on it, and said " I'll meet you there at 11 AM tomorrow. Try to get some rest tonight."

Drew and Kay just sighed as they walked Dr. Cain to the door. The second the door shut behind him, they were in each other's arms, sobbing uncontrollably. After several minutes, the little bit of energy that they might have had, drained away. They headed, silently for the kitchen and two more steaming cups of coffee. They sat and sipped silently for what seemed like an eternity, when Kay finally whispered to her frightened husband "I remember when I was Tara's age. I would wake up five out of every seven nights, because of a dream or nightmare. Oh Lord! Drew, is this somehow my fault? You know, genetics or some of all that other weird stuff!"

Immediately, Drew met her frightened gaze and replied, calmly "I hardly think that bad dreams are somehow hereditary, but it still wouldn't be your fault. You are an excellent Mother and Tara's best friend. I refuse to believe it's anyone's fault. They are only dreams after all, and Tara is afraid, but a dream can't really hurt her."

Kay sighed heavily, "I guess you're right honey, but it's so frustrating to not be able to help our daughter."

"Come now sweetie, let's go to bed. We could both use a good rest."Andrew suggested gently as he took Kay's hand and led her to their room.

"Please, Andrew, tell me everything is going to be alright with our little Angel." Kay pleaded with her husband for some kind of reassurance. Kay knew only too well about these types of dreams Tara was having, as she had experienced the same thing as Tara, at roughly the same age.

"Kay Honey, you know yourself that these are only dreams and cannot really hurt anyone." Andrew said in his most soothing voice he could muster. "Didn't you have bad dreams when you were Tara's age?"

"I guess you're right. I seem to be okay now, even though I had similar dreams. It's just what Mother used to tell me about my dreams that is really bothering me." Kay responded in almost a whisper.

Chapter 3

At 7:15 the next morning, the sun seemed almost too bright for the way Kay was feeling. As Kay silently crept across Tara's bedroom floor, the sun was just bleaching the entire colour out of the room, with its brightness. She reached Tara's bedside and gently sat in her rocker that she always kept there. Kay turned her gaze to her sleeping child and noticed Tara's eyes moving rapidly, under her eyelids. They seemed to be darting back and forth. Dr. Cain had explained to them, already about REM (Rapid Eye Movement) as the phase of sleep where the majority of our dreams occur. Kay's heart leapt into her constricting throat and her breathing became very rapid. Kay knew all too well, the signs of an imminent terror attack. She had them as a child, and since Tara got worse the attacks had returned to torture Kay. Oh God, Tara, wake up, she thought over and over again. A moment later, Tara sat bolt upright in bed and in a very clear, mature voice, she stated, "Yes, my little one, I will protect you." She opened her eyes and stared at Kay as if for the first time. Her eyes were clouded with worry far beyond her years. Tara rubbed her eyes, shook her little head and asked "Hi, Mommy, is it time to go to the sleep hospital already?"

"No, my darling we still have time for one of Daddy's famous breakfasts." Kay managed to stammer, trying to hide her shock.

"Cool, blueberry pancakes, bacon and orange juice, right Mommy?" Tara grinned at Kay. They both knew she loved all those things.

"Go get washed, get dressed and I'll go see how Daddy is doing in the kitchen, ok? You come down as soon as you're ready, sweetie." Kay said, in the most carefree voice she could muster.

"Ok, Mommy." Tara beamed.

As soon as Kay entered the kitchen she started to shake uncontrollably. Drew ran to her and held her to him. "It'll all work out, honey. Please try to stay positive. Our Faith and love have gotten us this far. Please, Kay, I love you. Relax." he crooned as he gently rocked her in his arms.

After several minutes, Kay's breathing returned to almost normal. She stopped shaking, a little, and took one careful step backwards.

"Drew, I love you too, and I know we will get through all of this, whatever it is, and we'll be stronger for it." Kay was out of breath with emotion.

"Group hug!!" Tara shrieked as she flew into their arms, giggling.

Kay and Drew managed to retain their balance despite the force of her tiny body. They wrapped their arms around her as she wriggled her way in between them.

"Let's eat, before it gets cold." Drew announced a little reluctantly.

Except for Tara's constant chatter there was little conversation during their farewell breakfast. After breakfast, Kay climbed the stairs to collect their bags. She had packed last night when she could not sleep. All she had been able to think about was her own mother and how they both had these dreams as small girls. It seemed to Kay that her mother, Elizabeth had spent a great deal of time in this "Dreamland" place, and she was always the calm one, never in a panic. This had only scared Kay more as a girl, so she went as few times as possible, and now all she wished for was to spare her daughter the terrors she still could feel.

Many kisses and hugs were exchanged at the front door before they were finally on their way to the Sleep Centre. The drive was only two hours, and the sun was beaming in the cloudless summer sky. The day would have felt like a smile from Heaven itself, if not for the thought of their destination. The drive itself was uneventful, except for Tara's undeniable excitement. She felt special for having gotten out of school for the summer, early. She was intrigued by the mere thought of a Sleep Centre. It sounded so cool.

As they finally pulled into the long winding lane towards the Sleep Centre, Kay could not help thinking that it looked more like a sprawling 18th century estate or mansion. It had all the original architectural features, landscaping and old-world charm. More like a honeymoon destination than a scientific sleep hospital. It was comforting and mysterious at the same time. There seemed to be a familiarity about this setting. But before Kay could really ponder this notion, they were at the front door and Dr. Cain was waiting on the steps.

"Good morning, ladies. How are my two favourite beauties on this lovely, southern day?" Dr. Cain asked, grinning.

"Fine, Doc." responded Tara, in a rush. "What a cool place for a hospital. This is like the house Seth, and I live in, in Dreamland," she continued, excitedly. "Is it the house?" she asked and then started to laugh. Even the idea was silly, Seth lived in Dreamland not on Earth, Tara thought to herself.

Dr. Cain was babbling about something or other. Tara heard rooms and menus, and then she heard them mention schedules and staff. Suddenly Tara just blurted out "So, where's the dungeon, Doc?" She was beginning to get a scary feeling here. It was almost like there were so many hidden secrets, evil ones, and here in this house.

She didn't know if she wanted to stay one night here, let alone a few weeks.

"Don't be silly, Tara, there is no dungeon here. This is a scientific facility, to help people, not a prison." Kay managed to say out loud. It was not how she was feeling She could also feel the evil that permeated this place, she really missed her mother right now.

By lunchtime Tara had already done a once over of the lower floor. On the first floor, in the front, the Sleep Centre was like a regular old house. In the back, though, where no one could see, there were hospital rooms and supply closets like the hospital her grandmother had been in before she went to Heaven. The front had a huge kitchen with two cooks and a giant refrigerator. The living room had a fireplace, huge windows and overstuffed chairs. There were also a bunch of smaller rooms that were mostly bedrooms and one huge bathroom.

The back, hospital part, even smelled like her grandmother. Grandma used to have pretty cool dreams. She used to tell Tara about them whenever Tara's mother wasn't around. Grandma said that the dreams were her own private Angel messages. She would think about a question or a problem when she was just about to go to sleep and ask God to send her the answer in her dreams. She always got the answer, so she was always calm and cool.

"Mommy!" Tara blurted out. Then realized that her mother and Dr. Cain had been talking. "Sorry, Mommy. I just wanted to ask a question." Tara continued.

Dr. Cain spoke next. "Go ahead, my dear. Ask whatever you want to."

"OK," Tara started, and then took a deep breath. Mommy always got weird when Tara asked about her grandmother's dreams. "Remember Grandma's dreams?" Tara's voice trailed off on the last word when she saw the look on her mother's face.

This was the first Dr. Cain had heard of Grandma's dreams and his interest was more than a little piqued. Dr. Cain chose his next words extremely carefully. "Ok, ladies. Let's have it," he said tentatively. "We can't have any secrets, especially family ones, if we're going to help Tara." He was trying very hard to conceal his excitement at this new development.

"Well, "Kay began. "My mother, Elizabeth, had lots of dreams in her day. She always called them messages from God's 'Angels'," Kay took a deep breath and continued. "I've had several dreams lately myself. Not like Tara's, but usually about Tara. Mother always called Tara, her little Angel." Kay sighed. "Some of the older people Mother used to know said she had a special gift from God. She could calm anybody down in no time at all. She helped a lot of her friends solve their problems with her dream ability." Kay looked at Dr. Cain and waited for him to call her crazy.

"Very interesting, Kay" Dr. Cain began. "Please tell me whatever you can remember about your mother's dreams." he said a little too eagerly for Kay's liking.

"Well, I have tried to forget them. Most of it just gave me the creeps anyway." Kay began, tentatively.

"You mean, they give you the "whooies", right Mommy?" Tara interrupted excitedly.

"Now, Tara, please. The Doctor only wants to hear about the dreams not the way that Mommy feels about them." Kay scolded.

"Please, Kay, continue." Dr. Cain asked, gently.

"Well, ever since I was very small, I can remember my mother never worried about anything. She would always say, "We'll ask God to send us his Angels to help us find the answer." She was a very religious woman. She said that every dream has a hidden message and that the place called Dreamland was, in fact, a real place. In Dreamland, all of our dreams and nightmares live in harmony. I always thought it was just a story she made up so that my dreams wouldn't scare me. She made it sound almost like Disneyland." Kay was getting stressed just from talking about her mother's dreams. and the strain was evident in her shaky voice.

Dr. Cain could see Kay was getting stressed just talking about her mother's dreams and the strain was evident in her face and shaky voice. Dr. Cain patted Kay on the hand and said, gently "Why don't you go and have a short nap to revive yourself. Tara and I will stay here and chat."

Kay was going to resist but she realized that she was exhausted so she reluctantly agreed. "Yeah, I am feeling a bit tired from the drive. I think I will have a short nap." Kay mumbled as she slowly rose from the table and headed for her room. "Don't talk Dr. Cain's two ears off, completely." Kay scolded as she gently kissed Tara's cheek, on her way out of the room.

Tara giggled playfully and looked Dr. Cain in the eye and said. "OK, Doc, what do you want to talk about?"

"Well," Dr. Cain began "Why don't you tell me what you can remember about your grandmother's dreams."

"Ok, Doc, but get ready for some really weird stuff." Tara warned, giggling. Tara began in her best scary voice "Grandma told me that the night before I was born, she had one of her best dreams ever. She said that she dreamt about me. She called me her special Angel, and she dreamed about me having even better dreams than her. She told me all about Dreamland and how there is a Dream keeper named Zorlak, and he's in charge of the whole land. He has Division Masters to run each section of Dreamland. Grandma told me it was all as real as here is." Tara took a deep breath and went on. "She said that when we sleep, we go there, but that's the only time we are allowed through." Tara stopped to catch her breath. She had been talking really fast, for some reason. Maybe, she talked fast because she was excited about Dreamland.

Dr. Cain took this opportunity to ask Tara some questions about her own dreams now that they were alone. "What do you usually dream about, Tara?" Dr. Cain asked.

"All kinds of cool stuff, Doc." Tara replied off handed.

"Ok, Honey. What kinds of cool stuff?" Dr. Cain continued, undeterred.

"Well, after my grandma died and went to Heaven to help God, I saw her in Dreamland." Tara sighed.

"How could she be in Dreamland, Tara?" Dr. Cain asked, cautiously.

"Oh, sorry about that. God can send people there when they get to Heaven, but only if their spirits are ready. That's why Grandma's there to help the Dream keeper. He needed help keeping everybody calm." Tara replied, as Dr. Cain should have already known that.

"Oh, I see." replied Dr. Cain. "But, Tara, what did the Dream keeper need your grandmother for?" Dr. Cain was starting to get a very uneasy feeling in the pit of his stomach.

"I just told you. To calm everybody down. Grandma was always really good at that. She could even keep Mommy calm. She said it was her special gift from God." I guess that's why God sent her to Dreamland." Tara sighed.

"How long was your grandma there for, in Dreamland?" Dr. Cain asked hesitantly.

"Oh, she's still there." Tara said. "Do you want me to ask her what's going on there? I will tonight if you want me to." Tara asked sincerely.

Dr. Cain's heart jumped into his throat. Could this little girl be serious? Could she go to sleep and talk to her dead Grandmother in her dreams? "Yes." was all Dr. Cain managed to croak out of his constricted voice box. Then he quickly added "If it's okay with you, Honey?"

"It's alright by me, but don't tell Mommy whatever you do, she'll go ape. She gets all weird and stuff whenever I talk to Grandma. She's afraid that someone or something in Dreamland is going to hurt me, but Grandma's there now. It's not like before when Mommy went, it was really scary back then. My Grandma told me that she wouldn't let any of "them" hurt me." Tara finished in a very matter of fact fashion.

"Who are "they"?" Dr. Cain asked immediately.

"Oh, the nightmare fairies. They're the bad ones in Dreamland. They scare people who go there in dreams, and they try to make them turn bad. Grandma already told them all to leave me alone because God said so. Mommy thinks that Grandma was crazy and I think she's scared that I'm turning into a crazy person too." Tara sighed.

Dr. Cain tried as hard as could to get more information from Tara, but she was becoming a little distracted. "How many others are there in Dreamland? Are they all people like your grandma? Could I meet any of them?" He persisted.

"Mommy should get up now. I'm hungry." Tara announced out of nowhere as she leapt to her feet to search for her mother.

Dr. Cain resigned himself to waiting for further insight into all this talk of Dreamland as he rose to follow Tara in her search for her mother. His mind was reeling with this new information he had already gotten from Tara. He had to find a way into Dreamland, but how? If only Tara could get him in there, he could gather some information to further his sleep research, as well as his once floundering dream research.

Chapter 4

Kay snuggled under the down filled comforter in the room that Dr. Cain had given her. It was a sterile room, like in a hospital, but the bed was a wonderful feather bed. The feather mattress was encased in flannelette and the lamp on the nightstand was stained glass. Everything in the entire room was antique, as if it had always been in this house. Dr. Cain had left a leather-bound journal on the nightstand along with a couple of nice pens. On the opposite wall from the bed was an antique chest of drawers with a small wardrobe on top. They had painted all of the furniture white, "What a shame" Kay thought "It must have been beautiful when it was in its original state." The wall at the foot of the bed had two huge full-length mirrors on it. Kay thought it was probably a two-way mirror so they could watch her sleeping. That thought immediately gave her the creeps. She was so drained from the drive and all the talk of dreams that she was asleep in minutes. The minute she dozed off she could feel herself falling. With a soft thud she landed, she looked around and saw clouds, as far as the eye could see. Kay knew she was dreaming but couldn't wake herself up. She hated her dreams because they had always terrified her.

"Kay, Honey, relax, don't be afraid Momma's here." Elizabeth whispered gently in Kay's ear.

"Momma, you're dead. Where am I? How are you here? Oh God! please let me wake up." Kay begged.

Elizabeth continued, quietly. "Kay, my love, there is nothing to fear. You're in Dreamland with me…"

"No!" Kay screamed at her dead Mother. "There is no such thing as Dreamland!" Kay sounded like a frightened child now. "You made it up. It's just a bedtime story!"

"Calm down, Dear. Relax and listen carefully. It's for your own good, and Tara's." Elizabeth spoke to Kay in that annoyingly calming voice she had all of Kay's life, only this time Kay could barely hear her mother. She heard the urgency in her mother's voice better than her actual words. The tone itself sent a chill up Kay's spine.

"Momma, please! What does Dreamland have to do with Tara, or me, for that matter? How come I can see and hear you?" Kay was starting to calm down a little bit but was still totally bewildered.

"There are certain Dreamers that are selected as helpers. They each have a special quality that is needed here. Dreamland is actually a parallel universe just like the Earth, and it is all within God's realm. There is no more to be afraid of here than in your real world, dear. God picks Dreamers for these special gifts. I was chosen to help calm the dwellers here during this very difficult time, especially. When Dreamers first get selected, they are all afraid until they learn and understand what is expected of them. My gift is to calm people, like when I was alive." Elizabeth finished

"So, why am I here then? I have always been terrified of Dreamland." Kay asked haltingly, dreading the answer she knew was coming.

"Well, partly for you and partly for Tara." Elizabeth stated.

"What special gifts do we have that they could possibly need here?" Kay was getting upset all over again.

"What do you mean?" Kay demanded.

"I can't explain it right now. We have to hurry!" Elizabeth said.

"Hurry? Where? Why? Mother, you are not making sense again." Kay scolded.

"Just follow me." Elizabeth said sternly as she rose and took Kay's hand in hers.

As they walked briskly through the clouds, Kay could feel a floor under them. She was grateful for the floor, as she was not up to walking on clouds at the moment. They seemed to be in a long corridor now and Kay could barely make out a door up ahead. She always thought her mother was a bit crazy, but now she was convinced. This whole dream was insane. As they neared the door Kay got more nervous. Now what? She thought to herself. Tara usually had dreams like this, not her. What was going on? Before Kay could even fully formulate that question in her mind, the door in front of them swung open on it's own, without a sound. Standing there was some kind of creature. He had a pointed nose and chin and black hair that was combed back so severely that it was like a crown. It almost looked like a racing helmet for a cyclist. He had elf ears and bristly, bushy black eyebrows. His eyes were an eerie green. They were like a bottomless pool of still spring water. His stare was unnerving; it was like he could see right through her.

There were little specks of gold throughout his eyes that seemed to have a life of their own. Kay hesitated at the door while her mother, Elizabeth and this creature exchanged pleasantries in a barely audible whisper.

"C'mon dear, time is wasting" Elizabeth said over her shoulder to Kay "We must hurry. That Doctor at the Sleep Centre will be waking you any moment."

"WHAT?? How did you even know about the Sleep Centre, Mother? Now you are really starting to scare me." Kay whined, to no avail.

"You must see this before he awakens you so you can help Tara. This entire experience is designed so you can help her more. You need to understand what is going on. Tara really needs you now and you must be strong, for her and for Drew." Elizabeth was trying everything to calm her daughter. "You must be open to everything now, or you cannot help your daughter. We didn't choose this path but we are on it and we must continue as best we can." Elizabeth trailed off. "Now is not the time to be skittish!" Elizabeth scolded.

Kay really didn't know how much more of this madness she could take right now, but she listened to her mother and followed her. She could tell by the tone in her mother's voice that there was no room for discussion. She followed her mother around a winding, wooden walkway. When Kay looked to her left all she saw was a darkened cavern that seemed endless and on her right side was a smooth rock wall. She felt a chill in the air and shivered at the dampness. Kay shivered so hard that she nearly lost her footing.

"Focus, Dear. We're almost there now." Elizabeth said soothingly without even turning around or missing a step.

It seemed to Kay that her mother was much more agile here than she had been when she was alive. What was she thinking? This was only a dream; of course, her mother would seem agile and ageless. This was a manifestation of her subconscious fears and concerns for Tara.

Out of nowhere, there came an eerie red glow. It was just like the one that had been around Tara's bedroom door the night before.

"Where in Hell are we, Mother!" Kay demanded in a harsh whisper.

"Shush!" Elizabeth whispered back, urgently. "They don't know we're here and I'd like to keep it that way for the time being."

Kay gazed around her with utter amazement. She could not believe her own eyes. How could this be? Was there really a parallel universe called Dreamland? Dear God! How? Why? What were all these creatures and why were they all here together? "Mother, what is this place and why did you bring me here?" Kay whispered.

"This is the central meeting place for all of Dreamland's Division Masters. "Elizabeth whispered cautiously. She knew, only too well, how much Kay hated even the mention of Dreamland, she always had.

"Ok, I saw it. Can we go now?" Kay's whispers were becoming more urgent by the minute.

"One more minute. You need to hear this." Elizabeth replied in an off-hand manner.

Suddenly, a huge creature sprang from the crowd and landed on what appeared to be a small stage in the middle of the crowded cavern. He was gnome like but had glowing red eyes and a jagged toothy grin. He appeared to have difficulty straightening to a fully erect stance. It was probably his oversized wings that hampered his movements.

He started pounding his huge fist on a podium and bellowed, "Now is our time. We must act before the child knows. We have found a weakness. We must destroy or be destroyed." Another crash of his huge fist was the last thing Kay heard just before she lost consciousness.

Chapter 5

When Kay opened her eyes Dr. Cain was standing over her looking confused and concerned. She nearly jumped out of her skin.

"How long have you been standing there?" Kay demanded.

"Just long enough to know you were having a lucid dream." Dr. Cain replied calmly.

Kay glared at him for a long moment then and didn't speak.

Dr. Cain spoke in an even voice "Would you like to tell me about it Dear, while it is still fresh in your mind?" Dr. Cain continued undeterred.

"No!" Kay snapped, "I have the journal you gave me to write my thoughts in. I'll just use that to record my memories of the dream. Thank-you." Kay ended tersely.

This was one of the first dreams Kay had remembered in a very long time and she preferred to keep it to herself, at least for the time being. She was still unnerved by her mother's warning to stay 'open to anything'. It had been nice to see her mother again, even if it was in a dream. Kay was not yet ready to share the details of her dream, especially with Dr. Cain. She was starting to get a very bad 'vibe' from him ever since they had arrived at the Sleep Centre. Her mother's tone when she spoke of Dr. Cain waking Kay up sent a chill through her. Kay was starting to wonder if she was going crazy, just like she had always thought her mother had. After all, the old adage went "like mother, like daughter"

Suddenly, Kay realized she really didn't know very much about Dr. Cain or his field of study. What was he hoping to learn from all of these sleep studies and dream analysis tests anyway? She heard Dr. Cain clear his throat and she immediately became aware of the fact that she had been staring at him, not speaking.

Dr. Cain spoke first "Are you alright, Kay?" He asked with genuine concern in his voice. "You look like you've seen a ghost," he continued.

"What, exactly, is it you do here, Dr. Cain?" Kay asked more impatiently than she intended to, but far less frustrated, than she felt.

"Well, we measure the speed of eye movements during sleep to determine the frequency, duration and number of REM stages per night. With Tara, we will also monitor her blood pressure, heart rate, pulse, breathing and brain wave activity during sleep." Dr. Cain spoke in a rehearsed tone of voice.

Before he could continue, Kay asked "And what, exactly, do you use all the data for? What can it tell you? Surely, you can't view a persons dreams can you?" Kay took a deep, cleansing breath and prayed to God that Dr. Cain hadn't seen her most recent dream, even though she didn't know why, yet.

"Well, we've been developing a technique to do just that. It's a kind of monitor that we connect to an EEG machine, electroencephalograph, to monitor brain activity. We record all the brain waves and transfer them to another computer graphics program to unscramble the messages. Eventually we hope to be able to add video images." Dr. Cain's voice was animated, and Kay could see a gleam in his eyes.

No wonder her mother had such contempt in her voice when she spoke of him.

Kay's Mother, Elizabeth, had always been a purist. She was a staunch believer in good and evil. She had always known in her heart that eventually good will triumph over evil. Elizabeth also believed that certain areas of existence should never be tampered with. Dreamland had always been one of those areas her mother had protected vigorously. Kay didn't know if it was her recent dream or not, but she felt calmer and more open to anything. Her Mother still could control her from the grave, or Dreamland, wherever she really was. Kay had always been an obedient child but never very adventurous. Maybe, all she needed was some guidance and input from her mother. After all, her mother had ordered her to be more open to the possibilities that existed all around her. For the first time in her life, Kay was actually optimistic and anxious for a new adventure.

Suddenly, Kay missed Drew more than she could remember ever having missed him before. He was always trying to get her to be more optimistic and adventurous. He would certainly be proud of her newfound interest in a new adventure.

"Where is Tara, Dr. Cain?" Kay asked. She had only just realized she hadn't heard her daughter's voice since she had awoken.

"Wakey, Wakey, sleepy head!! I'm hungry." Tara shrieked as she bounded onto Kay's bed to hug her. "Mommy, I've been everywhere. What a cool place. You were right, no dungeon." Tara rattled on.

"Yes, dear, it's lovely here, so peaceful. Now let's go see what the cooks have in store for our dinner. I'm hungry too." Kay said, smiling at her daughter.

Dr. Cain was still standing beside the bed with his mouth open and a dazed look on his face. He seemed surprised that Kay, suddenly, was not open to communicate the content of her own dreams, to him. Kay looked from Dr. Cain's face to Tara's and felt a small degree of control, finally. This was a definite improvement from her previous feelings of chaos, confusion and bewilderment. Her Mother had straightened her out again, this time from "beyond". Somehow this, only comforted, did not surprise Kay. Kay knew that this newfound confidence was a fragile thing and if she was to dwell on where her mother had told her she was, the feelings of panic and fear would return, full force. Kay decided not to think about her dream anymore, at least for now.

She reached down for her daughter's hand and cheerfully quipped, "Last one to the table is a rotten egg!"

Tara and Kay raced from the doorway to the kitchen with Dr. Cain following very slowly behind them. He seemed to be still pondering the sudden shift in Kay's attitude and demeanour.

"What surprises lay in store for us here, Mrs. Prescott?" Dr. Cain mumbled to himself.

Dinner passed quietly by, without incident. Kay and Tara chatted, as Dr. Cain remained lost in his own thoughts.

"What in Heavens name is wrong with you, Dr. Cain? You look like a storm cloud moving in from the north." Kay teased, gently.

"Mama!" Tara exclaimed. "That's what Grandma always said about your face whenever she talked about Dreamland. Oops, sorry Mama, I forgot." Tara's voice trailed off to a whisper.

"Oh, Tara, honey, don't be silly. We're here to talk about your dreams, Dreamland and anything else that might help you get better." Kay said soothingly.

"I'm not sick, Mama. I only have bad dreams." Tara said in her own defence.

The balance of the evening was spent in front of a roaring fire in the den. Each of them was lost in their own thoughts and not much conversation was to be had. Soon, it was time to bathe Tara and put her to bed.

Once Tara was safely tucked in, Kay went to her own room. She was anxious to write her thoughts and memories about her dream, in her journal Dr. Cain had given her earlier that day.

As Kay began to write down the details of her experience with her mother earlier in Dreamland, it occurred to her that this had been a childhood terror of hers, the mere mention of Dreamland sent her into screaming fits, and her mother could barely get her calmed down.

This time Kay needed to be strong for her daughter, Andrew and her mother. Hopefully, this madness would soon end, forever.

Kay didn't realize then that this was her and her daughter's destiny as it had been her mother's and she could not change any of it. It was never really going to go away, at least not anytime soon. Kay wrote for a long time and described in detail the surroundings and creatures she had seen with her mother in Dreamland. She shuddered when she pictured Zorlak and how huge he was. How could this even be a real place. No one had ever heard of it except her mother and she had always been sworn to secrecy. Little did Elizabeth know, but Kay never wanted to tell anyone about the nightime visits to an unreal, but real place. She had been teased enough in school for being different from the other school children. She never really did figure out why they saw her as different, but her mother always said it was because she was a special child and the other children just didn't understand that. So, Kay just accepted it as her cross to bear and moved on. Kay thought about other dreams she had over the years and started to remember more details than she had ever been able to identify before.

When Kay finished writing, she had a sudden feeling of fear pass over here. She knew then that she did not want Dr. Cain to read what she had written, so she tore out the pages and hid them in her clothing.

Shortly thereafter she slipped into an exhausted sleep, dreamless she hoped.

Chapter 6

Tara had already made up her mind that she was going back to find Seth. She had to make sure he was still all right. She could hardly wait to fall asleep and go back to the old house where she and Seth lived. As soon as Kay left her room, Tara started preparing herself to return to Dreamland. She lay very still and quiet, closed her eyes and thought about Seth as hard as she could. Tara wanted to go back into her dream, but before they left the den. She needed to find out where it was, when it happened and what those loud noises had been.

It wasn't very long before Tara was floating and flying over familiar rooftops, in her flowing, white, angelic gown. Then, there she was, in the den with the old dress on and staring out that huge window. She could hear whimpering from the overstuffed chair in front of the fire. Tara turned, slowly, from the window and the room was exactly as she remembered it. This time she would be ready for Seth's lunge into her arms.

"Mama!" Seth cried as soon as their eyes met, Seth leapt from the chair into Tara's arms. This time Tara was ready. They still both landed in the overstuffed chair behind Tara, giggling.

"Seth, honey, Mama needs to ask you some important questions. They may sound silly, because I already know the answers, but please answer them anyway, Ok?" Tara rocked him gently in her arms as she spoke.

"Ok, Mama, like a game, right?" Seth asked innocently.

"Yes, my love, like a game." Tara replied. "Ok, first, what year is it?" she asked shyly.

Seth burst out laughing and replied "Mama, this really is silly. You know it's 1864. Next, you're going to ask me where we live." Seth took one look at Tara's face and realized she didn't know where they lived. Now, he was getting scared. She must have lost all her memories when she had the Fever, he thought.

Tara saw the sudden fear in his little face. So, she immediately scanned the room for clues. Tara knew that the fear Seth felt was only going to escalate if she didn't act fast. There had to be something, she knew it was an old southern house, because of the size. The clothes, boots and furniture attested to the year, 1864.

Suddenly, it came to her; they lived in Atlanta, Georgia. Tara sighed as she said, "Seth, I know we live in Atlanta, Georgia, silly."

Now the loud noises made sense to Tara. The noises were gunfire, and they were coming closer. Maybe there were soldiers in the attic, already. After all, she had just gotten there. The house was on a large knoll, at the base of Kennesaw Mountain, overlooking Atlanta. Tara thought maybe the small, antique door and winding staircase led to some kind of a bomb shelter. She had very little time to get Seth to safety, judging from her last visit.

Bang!! There it was, the first crash. Tara jumped to her feet, spilling Seth onto the floor. She bent down, grabbed his hand and exclaimed, "Ok, Seth, it's time for a little adventure."

"To the shelter!" Seth announced, in his best grown up voice.

This time Tara knew exactly what to do, so without wasting a moment, she dragged Seth down the hall toward the small, antique door. She remembered exactly where it was, and she knew there was an oil lamp beside it. They were through the door of the shelter and on the stairs in less than two minutes. The cast iron stairs swayed beneath their weight and Tara could see the faint image of suspension wires above them. Tara shook her head; she didn't think that suspension cables had been invented in 1864. She didn't have any time to ponder this now, because the stairway seemed to be collapsing under their feet. It was turning into a slide and there they were, sliding downward, hand in hand.

There was a red, eerie glow emanating from the bottom of what appeared to be a huge pit. As they slid closer to the red glow, Seth said, with sheer terror in his voice "Mama, are we going to hell?"

"No, my little darling. We are not going to hell. This is the adventure that I promised you. Don't be afraid, just hold Mama's hand tight." Tara hoped she sounded a whole lot calmer than she felt. Tara had no idea where they would end up, but she hoped her grandmother would show up soon to guide her.

With a sudden thump, they landed in a heap on top of each other. As they looked around them, Tara could see that they had landed on some kind of stone ledge. Straight ahead of them, she could barely make out the outline of a small door.

"Mama, that was fun. Can we do it again? Please?" Seth exclaimed excitedly.

"No, sweetheart, we must continue on our journey, our adventure is only just beginning." Tara said trying to sound excited.

They carefully picked their way, along the narrow path, toward the door. Tara edged it open, cautiously and to her relief there was a huge room behind it. The room was full of women and children. This must be the safe place her grandmother had told Tara about. Seth would be safe here. Now, Tara could continue her own dream exploration, and not worry about Seth.

Tara gave Seth a big hug and told him to go play with the other children. Now with him occupied, Tara snuck out of the room, back onto the path, to explore her surroundings. As she wandered along the path, she was nervous, but she knew she would be safe here.

Her Grandmother had always talked about Dreamland as a safe place for all of them. Suddenly, Tara realized that she was her 7-year-old self again as she searched for her Grandmother. Before this realization could fully take shape, Tara felt a huge, cold hand settle on her left shoulder.

"Are you lost, little one?" a hoarse, raspy voice boomed in the dark, red glow.

"No. I'm just looking for my...eh" she trailed off. Tara had remembered her grandmother's warning not to expose her identity unless she was with her. "...My friend, Elizabeth." she finally finished, looking up at this strange creature. She almost fell when she saw it. It had a human body and huge wings. Its hands were larger than it's head and it was funny neon blue.

"Who are you?" Tara asked.

"I am Yarong, keeper of the path," the creature answered proudly.

"I watch for strangers and help the lost ones find their way back to the fold." he finished.

"Well, I am looking for the old woman, they call Elizabeth. Can you help me find her?" Tara asked cautiously.

"Then you are a lost little one, after all?" Yarong asked curiously.

"Yes, I guess I am then." Tara answered timidly.

"Miss Elizabeth is on level four with the other new arrivals. You should have stayed closer to your group. Then you wouldn't be lost. No matter. Follow me, little one and I shall lead you back to your fold." Yarong stated in such a way, Tara knew she wasn't the first lost little one to stray.

Tara followed, obediently, relieved that she hadn't blown it. She could hardly wait to see her grandmother again.

Chapter 7

Kay was having a great deal of difficulty falling asleep. She figured that she was only a little nervous at the prospect of visiting Dreamland, again. She was missing Drew even more, now. Kay decided to make some notes in the diary that Dr. Cain had left on her nightstand, earlier. As she began writing she was struck by the realization that Dr. Cain would read it whenever she slept. Kay was determined to write in the old, coded language she had shared, as a child, with her mother. Dr. Cain would never be able to decipher this code. It was made up of all the secrets she and her mother had shared. Even her grandmother, Charlotte, had never been able to decode it.

She had only written a few lines when she began to drift off to sleep, reluctantly.

Kay suddenly realized she was in Dreamland. The large room was well lit and teeming with women and children. The sense of safety was overwhelming. Kay had never ever felt that safe before. It almost glowed with serenity, comfort and peace. This convinced her that her mother had sent for her and would, no doubt, appear whenever she was ready.

As she waited for her mother, Kay wandered through the throngs of happily playing children. She was watching them play unaware of her presence when she heard a small child shriek with excitement. "Seth, stop it. That tickles!"

Kay, deep in her own thoughts, turned, slowly toward the direction of the voice. The only thought pounding in her head was "Could this be the same Seth from Tara's dreams?" Kay decided to make her way through the crowded centre to see Seth, up close.

She had only made it about twenty feet closer to the voice when she felt a firm hand settle on her left shoulder. She whirled around with such speed she almost fell over. Much to Kay's relief it was her mother, finally, with a very impatient smile on her face.

"Mother! Why am I here? Is that the same Seth from Tara's dreams? How can all this be happening? Why can't I speak to Seth?" Kay's questions came out in a torrent of words.

Her mother raised one hand to silence Kay and said, "All will become clear to you very soon, Kay. Now, please be patient and follow me."

Elizabeth turned, abruptly to leave and Kay followed her, obediently. They crossed the large centre full of women and children to a small door and out into a darkened hallway. The hallway smelled like damp musty towels mixed with old moss. The walls of it were made of curved stones placed in ancient mortar. As they wound their way further down the descending hallway, Kay could not even imagine what her mother had in store for her.

Elizabeth stopped so abruptly that Kay bumped into her. When they both regained their balance, Elizabeth pulled a skeleton key out of her apron pocket, put it in a tiny keyhole in the door. Kay could not even see the keyhole, but suddenly the door flew open and banged against the wall inside the room behind it. Kay was so awestruck all she could do is gape.

The door had been invisible to her, but her mother had no problem locating it amongst the smooth stones of the wall. The wall was so dark, and it curved around the spiral hallway, making Kay feel like she was in a cylindrical cave. How her mother had even found the door was a mystery to her, but then again, so was everything else even remotely related to Dreamland.

Elizabeth continued to lead Kay through a large room then small hallways and progressively smaller rooms. The rooms varied between no lights, dimly lit all the way to brightly lit. Finally, they entered a huge cavern. This was only dimly lit by lanterns hung on the stonewalls. The dankness could be felt. Kay's skin was starting to crawl with the mere thought of all that could be in here. They began to weave around stone carvings of figures Kay had only imagined. There were huge stone blocks everywhere, ready to be carved. Trapdoors seemed to be increasing in number and rope ladders going up to a ceiling that could not even be seen and down through holes in the floor near the walls. Kay's attention was brought back to the task at hand, suddenly as her mother stopped to open another 'invisible door' in the wall.

They passed through the door, silently and stopped. There in front of them was the ugliest creature Kay had ever seen, awake or asleep. Elizabeth grabbed Kay's hand, immediately. This served two purposes, one to get Kay to stop and the other to make sure she was silent. This 'monster' had a human body, huge hands, giant wings and it was an eerie shade of neon blue. His eyes glowed red and his voice was hoarse and raspy. Before Kay could even catch her breath, she heard her mother speak to the creature.

"Greetings, Yarong. I see you have brought me another lost little one. Well done."

"Yes, and thank-you Miss Elizabeth. I must return to my rounds on the path. God be with you, Ma'am." Yarong replied and was gone in a blink.

"Tara!!" Kay screamed. "How did you get here? Mother, tell me right now what is going on?" Kay was almost hysterical now.

"In here." Elizabeth said in a near whisper as she slowly, silently opened a 'door' Kay had assumed was another statue. As the stone statue door, creaked to a close, behind them Kay looked around in utter amazement.

"This is my private quarters." Elizabeth announced proudly. "In here we can speak freely. It was one of my conditions. Well, Tara it appears that your mother is now ready to discuss our little world." She continued in a teasing tone.

Tara giggled and said "Grandma, this is so cool. All of us together here, finally. Mama, are you ok?" Kay had not uttered a word in some time and Tara and Elizabeth were getting concerned. The two cohorts led Kay to an overstuffed chair so she could catch her breath.

Kay caught her breath and voice very quickly. Just as they quietly waited for the steady stream of questions to begin. "Mother, I really need to know why I am here, why Tara is here, why you are here and more importantly where is 'here'?"

Elizabeth, unfazed announced that she would get some tea and snacks and then start explaining. She disappeared behind a partial wall and re-emerged with tea, cookies and juice and all within a split second. Kay was far too pre-occupied to even be amazed by anything her mother could do now.

Elizabeth took a deep breath sat down and said "Now, Kay you should remember why we are here from your last visit. We do not have very much time. We must decide on an immediate course of action." Elizabeth continued, "Now, the problem is Lutharious. He has found a weakness in the fibre of time that keeps Dreamland

and Earth separate. He has decided that now is the time to be proactive and attack before Earth has a chance to attack Dreamland. This action cannot be permitted, and we must find a way to stop it, immediately. It would mean the end of both worlds, forever." Elizabeth was flushed with emotion and her voice shaking when she finally stopped for breath.

Kay was dumbfounded. She just sat there with her mouth open, and her gaze fixed on her mother.

Tara spoke first "Ok, Gram, what do they need us to do?" she asked in a much stronger voice than Kay had ever heard her use. She sounded like that adult that woke up in her body after her last vivid dream.

"Well, Tara..." her grandmother began. "We need to figure out what we can do to help." she trailed off.

"Do you know where this weakness is, Mother?" Kay asked, tentatively.

"Actually", Kay we do have our scouts out working on it. They are following Lutharious, from a safe distance, to determine how many residents know where the weakness is. I think it is probably only Lutharious that knows. In the interim, we need to discuss some other issues, Kay."

Kay could not imagine how much more there could possibly be to this madness.

Chapter 8

Kay knew, instinctively that she was not going to like what her mother had to say next. Years of lectures, life lessons and motherly advise had taught her that whenever her mother had that tone in her voice it was going to be a long speech.

Elizabeth got comfortable in her chair and began "Dreamland has existed for centuries. It is all part of God's world no matter what religion you practice. It is a wonderful place. Have you ever heard of the 'house of souls' in any religion? Well, Dreamland is sort of an extension of that house of souls. Not all of us are needed again as new souls. Once we have learned what we were supposed to, then we get to 'retire' here." She drew in her breath and continued, "Recently, we have had a huge influx of what we call 'little ones'. These are the children from Earth that need to be saved, moved or protected. They are brought to that safe room you arrived in and sorted according to whether or not their mothers were able to come with them. The ones who arrive without an escort are paired up with other life units. They are safer here than they would be anywhere on Earth. We will keep them here for as long as is necessary."

Kay could not remain quiet any longer "Mother, this all sounds like the ranting of a maniac. How could this place exist and for what purpose? Not only that, but Tara is only seven years old, and I can't yet believe that it's real. How much help could the two of us possibly be?" Kay was becoming even more bewildered by the moment. She had to stay calm for Tara's sake.

Elizabeth looked up into her daughters frightened eyes and said "Kay, my love, there is absolutely nothing to fear from Dreamland."

"Mother! Come on, now. We are facing the annihilation of both Earth and Dreamland if the three of us don't come up with a plan to save the day." Kay could no longer contain her frustration with the entire situation.

"Now that we are all three, together, we have the power to conceive the perfect solution. We will need a great deal of assistance from the Dreamland residents. The plan must be conceived now, before it is too late. I can set the plan in motion once you and Tara safely return to Earth. You see every generation has had a child chosen to protect Dreamland, if necessary. Tara is the child that has been chosen for this generation. That is why her dreams are so vivid and memorable. Kay, you and I must assist in her education so she can fully develop her gift." Elizabeth was becoming more impatient with this time-consuming explanation.

"Do you know, Mother, what her gift is supposed to be?" Kay asked reluctantly.

"Well, it has been discussed at length in the inner exclusive and cloistered sanctum. This is where the Dream keeper, Zorlak meets with all of us. The name of this elite inner sanctum was Zenithia, as it was the highest source of all power in Dreamland. Zorlak is in charge of all of Dreamland and he must continuously monitor for potential threats. We decided that it was time to train Tara so that she can protect herself from the negative forces of both realms. She will have a succession of lucid dreams that will show her exactly who she can trust and who to be wary of. You, Kay will also have a series of lucid dreams that will help you to understand your role in all of this and how you can help Tara" Elizabeth finished with a heavy sigh.

"Well, I think it's cool!" Tara announced as if it was a big game. "This will be fun."

"How is Dr. Cain involved, Mother?" Kay asked apprehensively.

"Well, Dr. Cain means well, but if he unlocks the secrets of Dreamland from Tara's dreams before we can fully develop her gift, well, we could have a serious problem." Elizabeth answered hesitantly.

"So, it is in Tara's best interest for us to be less than candid about the content of her dreams, right? But Dr. Cain said he is developing a method of dream transcription to view Tara's dreams on a computer program. If he accomplishes that, then what?" Kay was getting scared again.

"Don't worry, dear, Zorlak has a plan already in place to slow down the good Doctor." Elizabeth replied.

"Mother, you know how much I hate dreaming and the mere thought of visiting Dreamland on a regular basis terrifies me." Kay was becoming increasingly nervous at this idea. "Maybe we should just go home and deal with all of this without the aid of Dr. Cain. Wouldn't it be safer that way?" Kay finished hoping her mother would agree with her latest idea.

"Well, Dear, as easy a solution as that sounds, I'm afraid it isn't that simple. Dr. Cain already knows too much about Dreamland. You and Tara are part of Zorlak's plan to slow him down. You will need to stay at the Sleep Centre for now until it is safe for you to return home." Elizabeth took a deep breath and continued. "Now Kay, they are only dreams that will teach you how to help your daughter not anything that will scare you. You will become more and more comfortable with them as they progress. You will not be expected to participate in anything that you are afraid of, but this process is the most efficient way to make sure we are all up to speed in the shortest possible time frame. Now we must hurry, Zorlak wants to speak with you before you leave. Follow me girls." Elizabeth announced.

Elizabeth stood up and headed for the door. Tara jumped up and immediately followed. Kay reluctantly rose from her chair and followed her daughter and mother from the room. They briskly moved through the maze of stone blocks and statues quickly arriving at the small door where they had entered. Before any real time had passed, they were back out in the musty, darkened hallway. This time they were heading upwards rather than down. Kay wasn't sure if this made her feel better or worse, but she reluctantly followed the procession. The trek seemed effortless for all three of them and Kay felt oddly comforted by this. The noises they heard, periodically made Kay's skin crawl. They alternated between animal sounds and hushed human voices, but Kay could not see anyone or anything in the shadows. The walls seemed to be almost alive with sounds but none of them could be understood or clearly defined.

"Here we are, girls!" Elizabeth announced triumphantly. She placed her palm on the wall and without hesitation it glowed green and opened.

"Zorlak, I would like for you to meet my daughter and grand daughter." Elizabeth offered proudly, to a huge darkened, shadowy figure. There was a rumble and then the figure seemed to be turning toward them. Kay was instantly terrified and Tara, just as instantly, was excited.

"Welcome to our realm Katherine and Tara. Elizabeth here has told us great things about you both. It is an honor to finally meet you in person. Now, there are a few things I must warn you about before you leave us." Zorlak continued, "You must always be protective of your identity. There are forces here that would do you harm if they knew who you were. They are followers of Lutharious and will tell him of your presence. The only time you can reveal yourself is in the presence of Elizabeth, the calming one. Only she can protect your identity until we are finished your training. Then all will be revealed to you as full-fledged residents of Dreamland." He paused and stared from Kay to Tara and back again. "Do you have any questions of an urgent nature that we should deal with at once?" he asked.

"How dangerous is it for Tara, here?" Kay asked without even realizing she had opened her mouth.

"Good, concern for you child first, excellent quality. That will assist you in your experiences here, Kay. The Throgs will constantly watch Tara. They are the protectors of the chosen one. They are everywhere but are never seen." Zorlak finished.

"Are they the voices, in the walls in the hallway, that I heard on our way here?" Kay asked curiously.

"Excellent!" Zorlak boomed.

Kay jumped at the force of his voice and urgently added "I'm sorry if I have spoken out of turn, but I heard strange noises on our way here."

"Kay, relax you did not speak out of turn. Tara, did you hear any noises on the way here?" Zorlak asked.

"No sir, I only watched the path for those tiny little wiggly things. But I didn't see any this time." Tara answered in a matter-of-fact tone.

"Good, then it has already begun. Kay your gift includes acute hearing and Tara's gift includes acute vision. You have started the process on your own. This is a very good sign. I am very pleased. "Zorlak finished.

Tara could see Zorlak better than her mother and grandmother could. Now she knew why. He was a huge mass of black cloaks with a large head. His head was shaped like a cone. It went backwards and up in a way that made it look like the wind was blowing it back. Tara was thankful that her mother could not see him as clearly as she could. Her mother was always nervous of Dreamland, and he was a bit scary looking.

"When does my training start Mr. Zorlak, Sir?" Tara inquired meekly.

Zorlak's body seemed to be shaking. Elizabeth could have sworn he was laughing but when he spoke there was no sign of mirth in his voice.

"You can call me Zorlak, Tara, no mister or sir is required. Your training will commence as soon as you get back to earth and begin dreaming again. Now, before you leave there is one more thing you must be aware of. This is the one thing that you must never forget. Never tell anyone about our plans or activities here. It is imperative that no earth dwellers are ever sure of our existence. It is only the chosen few that are fully aware of our realm and its activities. Now go, be safe and God be with you." Zorlak finished and with a gentle wave of his huge hand he was gone.

Chapter 9

Kay awoke in the morning with a feeling of dread. Had she only dreamt it or was it an actual place. Could all of this be real? How had they become involved in such a ridiculous situation? Her mother seemed to be the source of this dilemma. Had her mother always been involved with the events of Dreamland? How could Kay have been so blind to it for so long? As these thoughts were entering her head and milling about, she became aware of Dr. Cain's presence in her room.

"How did you sleep, Kay?" He asked softly.

Kay was startled by his voice and could only mutter "Fine, Doctor and you?"

"I slept like a baby, Kay. Thank you for asking." Dr. Cain continued "Are we ready to explore Dreamland today?" He finished and looked deep into Kay's eyes.

"I really don't know if I'm up to it today. Maybe we should check with Tara and see how she is feeling?" Kay answered.

"OK, let's go and see where the little one is this morning. Shall we?" Dr. Cain replied.

Kay was immediately struck by Dr. Cain's use of the term "little one". Had he already gained some insight into the terminology of Dreamland? As soon as this thought entered her head, Kay knew it was utterly ridiculous.

There was absolutely no way he could possibly know. It must have been just a coincidence. Her mother had preached to her over the years that there was no such thing as a coincidence. Man, her head was spinning. Kay felt like she was going crazy. All of these strange ideas in her head. In her head Kay was saying, " Shake it off, girl" over and over again, when Tara came sprinting into the room.

"Good morning!" Tara was singing as she danced around the room.

"Good to see that our lively little one slept well" Dr. Cain observed.

"Who are you calling little one? I'm a big girl." Tara demanded of Dr. Cain.

"It's just a figure of speech, dear." Dr. Cain quickly responded. A bit too quickly for either Kay or Tara's liking. They exchanged a quick glance, but both remained silent in front of "the good Doctor".

"Let's eat!" Tara was the first to break the growing silence.

"Great idea." Kay responded taking Tara's hand in hers and leading her from the room. As they walked towards the breakfast room Kay decided that she and her daughter needed some time alone today to discuss the events of the previous evening.

As they all took their seats, Dr. Cain started planning the day's activities.

As he started rambling off his idea of the perfect itinerary, Kay's thoughts drifted back to the previous nights' activities. How was she going to know what she was supposed to learn from each of these dreams her mother had said she would soon start having?

What if she misunderstood the content or message of these dreams and was unable to be of assistance to her innocent daughter? Kay knew that she was just being paranoid and she had to force herself to calm down or this would end up being a self-fulfilling prophecy.

Taking a deep breath, Kay finally spoke, "Well, Dr. Cain, I was thinking that maybe Tara and I could use some time alone together today. Just to get acclimatized to our new location. Maybe we could pack a picnic and go for a nice long walk in the woods?"

"Well, I was hoping to get started today, but if you really feel Tara needs the day to adjust, I guess I could busy myself with the new computer program I'm working on." Dr. Cain agreed, reluctantly.

"Great, then it's all set." Kay answered "We'll make our picnic right after breakfast." Kay finished.

"Kay, I'd like us to meet for about an hour or so when you and Tara return from your picnic, OK?" Dr. Cain asked tentatively.

"No problem, Doctor. I'm looking forward to it." Kay lied believably.

Really, all Kay was looking forward to was getting away from the "Good Doctor" for the day. Maybe, then she could think clearly about their huge job ahead. Kay was very anxious to talk to Tara and get her thoughts and feelings on Dreamland and the important task that lay ahead.

The grounds of the sleep centre were amazingly lush and green. The woods surrounding the complex were strewn with winding paths. The weeping willow trees hung like a canopy over the walking trails. Kay and Tara had packed their picnic lunch and set out right after breakfast, as planned. As they walked through the picture-perfect paths, hand in hand, they remained silent, lost in their own thoughts. It was a breathtaking day as the sun shone brightly from its perch high in the cloudless sky. A subtle breeze gently rustled the dainty leaves as the birds teemed with delicate song. Soon they came upon a mossy clearing surrounded by exquisite, majestic trees.

"This is it!" Tara shrieked. "It's the place where Seth and I went on picnics. Here Mommy!" She could barely contain her excitement.

"Ok, sweetie, we'll have our picnic here too then." Kay was a little concerned with her daughter's reference to an imaginary boy but shrugged it off as they had bigger fish to fry right now.

As Kay spread out their blanket on the moss, Tara was darting from one tree to another. She was talking to them as if they were alive and giggling as she ran. Kay remembered that her vision was sharper now and that she could probably see things Kay had no hope of viewing. Kay busied herself with her picnic unpacking and thought about her dream the night before. She had resigned herself to the very real possibility that her mother was right and that she must help her daughter release her strength and save Dreamland. Kay never imagined she, of all people, would be assisting to save the place she feared ever since childhood. Oh well, her daughter needed her and that was all she needed to know.

Chapter 10

Dr. Cain was suspicious about Kay's need to be alone with her daughter. Especially after she had refused to share what he knew had been a very lucid dream. How was he going to find out everything he needed to know about Dreamland if he couldn't get Kay to share her memories? The prospect of finding out the nature and content of Elizabeth's dreams had him more excited than he had been in years. If his research was correct, lucid dreaming ran in families. Kay appeared to be the type of person who repressed her abilities. The capability for a person to control their lucid dreaming ability was indicative of an extremely strong will. If Kay possessed this ability, she would be an interesting subject to monitor. He could learn a great deal from both of them. No matter how hard he tried to concentrate on the calculations for his computer program his mind wandered to thoughts of Dreamland. He felt an overwhelming need to find out all he could about it. As a scientist he was trained not to believe in imaginary places or people. The thought that Tara and Kay could communicate with Elizabeth in the here after was astounding. Tara had hinted at this possibility and Dr. Cain needed to get her alone to further investigate her experiences in Dreamland. The red glow around Tara's bedroom door also had Dr. Cain intrigued. Was it an emanation from another dimension or was it merely a hallucination of distraught parents? Only further research would answer these questions for him.

Dr. Cain decided to take a look at the journal that he had given Kay to record her thoughts and dreams in. As he entered her room, he was immediately struck by the feeling he was being watched. He bent slightly to retrieve her notebook from the nightstand and felt an almost imperceptible rush of cool air pass his right shoulder. As he straightened, he shivered from this breeze. He looked all around the room but could see nothing. Dr. Cain tucked the diary under his right arm and briskly headed for the door. As he reached for the doorknob the door slammed shut, with a bang. He jumped in sudden fear and all but ran the rest of the way to the door. Barely stopping to grasp the knob tightly he twisted the knob and threw open the door. His nerves jangling, he headed back to his lab to read Kay's notes. With shaking hands, he opened the diary and sat behind his desk. Confusion was his first reaction, because he didn't understand one word that was written on the diary's pages. Was it a foreign language or some kind of code? He poured over the diary pages for what must have been hours. When he finally returned the book to its rightful place his head was pounding, and his neck was stiff.

Dr. Cain didn't waste any time in Kay's room when he returned the diary because he was still confused and a little perplexed by his previous experience there. He felt that what he needed to do was make a list of the things he already knew about Kay, Tara, Elizabeth and Dreamland. He needed to make some sense out of all this, and soon. His research was going extremely quickly up to this point, and he was in no mood to have it falter at this crucial phase. Dr. Cain was becoming less interested in helping Tara get through her nightmares and more interested in investigating the existence of Dreamland. He was meeting with Kay when they returned and he would question her on Dreamland, her nightmares and her reluctance to share her lucid dream she had at the Sleep Centre.

All Dr. Cain knew about Dreamland so far was that Kay was terrified of the mere mention of it and Tara was excited by it. Tara had mentioned that her grandmother lived in Dreamland now because God needed her help to calm all of the residents there. Kay had explained that Dreamland was where all of our dreams and nightmares lived in harmony. To him, this sounded like a children's story and nothing more. It was strange, however that Tara and her grandmother both dreamed of this place. This Dream keeper named Zorlak was interesting too. Division Masters and Nightmare Fairies. It was all a little too unbelievable. Hearing it from a 7-year-old child made it even less believable. Tara had said that her mother, Kay used to go there when she was a little girl, but it wasn't safe, and she was scared. Kay did seem to be nervous about Dreamland and its inhabitants whenever her daughter brought it up. Dr. Cain would need to confirm the information Tara had given him by talking to Kay about it. Kay, although reluctant, would speak to him about it if he told her, it would help Tara. He didn't really know if it was to help Tara or him, but he knew he had to get to the bottom of this mystery before it drove him crazy.

Dr. Cain sat at his desk and for the first time since he graduated from medical school he could not concentrate. He knew that he needed to focus so that he could write down the questions he wanted Kay to answer when she returned. It suddenly struck Dr. Cain that Kay and Tara had been gone for hours. He wondered if they were having a good picnic. He hoped this outing would make Kay more receptive to his probing questions. Now all he had to do was figure out what he wanted to ask her. After dinner he would suggest that Tara turn in early so he and Kay could discuss her progress and the plan of action from here on at the Sleep Centre. It was a fact-finding exercise as well as a healing process for Tara.

Dr. Cain was so intrigued by Tara and her ability to communicate with her grandmother. He wasn't sure yet if it could be happening or was it all simply a lucid dream that was extremely complex in its very nature.

Dr. Cain could not ignore the presence of the red glow and all it's potential meanings. He knew there was definitely something he had never been exposed to ever before. His fervent hope was that he would be able to handle it whenever it happened, but he knew something big was afoot.

Chapter 11

"Mommy, look at these beautiful flowers over here." Tara squealed as she ran around their picnic blanket giggling.

"Tara, my love, you have to sit down for a moment. We have a great deal to discuss, and we can't do it at the Sleep Centre." Kay said in a mildly scolding voice.

"Ok, oh yeah, wasn't that creepy when Dr. Cain called me a "little one"?" Tara asked as she plunked herself down beside Kay.

"Yes, it was, but I don't think he knew what it meant. How much have you already told Dr. Cain about Dreamland?" Kay questioned.

"I told him that Grandma lives there because God needed her to go and keep people clam. I told him about Zorlak and the nightmare fairies too. Mommy, am I in trouble?" Tara was starting to sound concerned.

"No, sweetie, you aren't in trouble. We just have to make sure we don't tell him anything else. Ok?" Kay responded in the calmest voice she could muster. She was afraid that Dr. Cain already knew too much but she didn't want to alarm Tara.

"Is that everything you told him, honey?" Kay wanted to be sure.

"Yeah, Mommy, I promise." Tara answered brightly.

"Well, I think we can assume that Dr. Cain thinks this is just a children's story that your grandmother told us both. So, the first phase of our plan is to keep him thinking that Dreamland is only a fantasy and not real, Ok?" Kay finished breathlessly. She could feel the beginnings of their plan and she was starting to feel exhilarated by the whole idea of helping Dreamland.

"Ok, Mommy, I can do that. I can talk and talk until Dr. Cain thinks I'm crazy and that Grandma and I made it all up. Would that work?" Tara asked, beaming with pride at her good idea.

"That would be perfect, honey. Now, the next phase is what we have to discuss, Ok?" Kay asked, cautiously testing her willingness to continue.

"Just like Grandma said, right Mommy? "Tara asked innocently.

"Yes, that's right. Now, we need to try and figure out what the weakness in Dreamland is and how to fix it before Lutharious can do anything. We don't have very much time, but we are safer here at the Sleep Centre than we would be anywhere else right now. Do you have any ideas, Tara?" Kay asked.

"Well, I saw those little wiggly things on the path and Zorlak was happy I could see them. Maybe they know where the weakness is." Tara responded easily.

"Maybe they do know and can lead us there. Any other ideas of what the weakness could be. Is it in the liner or is it a person or thing?" Kay kept questioning her daughter.

"You are the one who spent the most time there. I wasn't able to stay when I was little because Grandma wasn't there to protect me. So, I am depending on your excellent memory to help me, Ok?" Kay finished.

"I remember hearing some weird noises around the door to the safe room when Seth and I went there. Maybe when I go back, I can listen harder. Or you could come with me, Mommy. That would be fun, Ok?" Tara concluded.

"Maybe we could go there tonight, and I may be able to figure out what the noises are. Great idea, Sweetie." Kay sounded a lot more excited at this idea than she felt. "I have to have a meeting with Dr. Cain for about an hour when we get back so we shouldn't stay out here too late." Kay reminded Tara.

"Ok, Mommy, I'll go to bed early, right after dinner. Then you and Dr. Cain can talk, and you can still go to bed early. I'll meet you at the safe room. Now, can we try to catch some butterflies?" Tara finished, now out of breath.

"Well, we can chase some butterflies, but remember, we can't catch them because it hurts their wings. Before we do that can you tell me how I get to the safe room in Dreamland?" Kay queried.

"Sure, I forgot you haven't been there as much as me, sorry. Well, just before you go to sleep think really, really hard about the safe room. Remember everything you can about what it looks like and who you saw there last time. Then, just close your eyes and I'll already be there thinking you through. It isn't hard Mommy; you can do it." Tara said encouragingly.

Tara's mention of who was in the safe room reminded Kay of Seth. Had she really seen him there? "Tara, honey, I saw a little boy playing with some other children the last time we were there, and his name was Seth. Is there any way it was the little boy from your dream at home?" Kay asked tentatively.

"Sure, it was him. I took him there so he would be safe. Where he lived, there was a war or something going on and I had to protect him." Tara said without batting an eye. "Now, let's play Mommy." she stated.

"Ok, let's gather up our picnic basket and blanket and we can chase butterflies on our way back to the Sleep Centre. It's starting to get late now." Kay said.

They silently gathered up all of their belongings. Kay hadn't realized how long they had been gone. It was now late in the afternoon. She could tell because the sun was starting to slide lazily from its previous spot high in the sky. If they didn't hurry it might be dark before they got back to the centre. Tara ran ahead of Kay, chasing butterflies. This had been a favorite pastime of hers too when she was Tara's age. She could remember long walks and picnics with her mother too. The language they had developed was partly a result of these long walks they had shared. The good memories from her childhood had been clearer since she had visited Dreamland. She wondered if this was all part of the plan to help her remember Dreamland. Was there something that had happened to her there so long ago that could help them now? Before she knew it, they were in sight of the Sleep Centre. Dr. Cain was standing on the front steps wringing his hands together. Kay wondered what was wrong with him. Had they been gone that long that he was worried about them?

"Dr. Cain!" Kay yelled across the yard. "Were we gone that long?" she asked, knowing full well that they had been gone most of the day.

"I was starting to get a little concerned. I was afraid maybe you got lost in the woods. But I see you are both well rested and happy. So, dinner is ready let's go eat before it gets cold, shall we?" Dr. Cain asked as he turned on his heel and entered the huge front door.

"Mommy, he looks like he saw a ghost. What is the matter with him? He didn't even hold the door open for us. Are we in trouble?" Tara asked with genuine concern in her voice.

"No, he was just getting worried. You know, like when Daddy is late coming home from work and Mommy is worried." Kay replied, realizing how much she missed Drew right now.

"Mommy, can we call Daddy on the phone? I really miss him today. He would have had fun on our picnic with us." Tara declared.

"Let's check with "the good doctor" shall we?" Kay responded with a giggle and a wink.

Chapter 12

Dinner passed quietly, with all three deep in their own thoughts. Dr. Cain was the first to speak, as he had eaten very little. "How was the picnic, ladies?" he asked tentatively.

"We found a really pretty clear spot in the woods with big trees around it. There was soft moss to sit on and flowers to smell. We even chased some butterflies on our way out." Tara finished breathlessly.

"Yes, we had a wonderful time, Doctor. We ate and rested and enjoyed each other's company." Kay relayed off hand.

"Good, so you are both refreshed and ready to get to work in the morning then. Kay, you and I can have our coffee in the study after dinner so we can talk." Dr. Cain finished.

"Mommy, can I go to bed now, before you and Dr. Cain talk. I'm pooped out." Tara asked sweetly.

Kay was beaming with pride as she got up from the table and took her daughter's hand. As she started to lead her daughter to her room, she said to Dr. Cain "You can get the coffee ready and I'll meet you in the study. Now, say goodnight to Dr. Cain, Tara."

"Night Doc!" Tara quipped over her shoulder as Kay led her from the room.

"See you in the morning, Angel." Dr. Cain responded without thinking.

"He called me Angel Mommy, just like Grandma does." Tara said a little surprised.

"Don't worry, darling. You are a little angel." Kay said in as calm a voice as she could muster. She was starting to become more suspicious of Dr. Cain's intentions daily. Her Mother's warnings were ringing in her ears almost constantly today. Kay was reluctantly beginning to believe that nonsense her mother had preached to her for years. Dreamland is a real place. It hit Kay like a slap in the face. She stopped, dead in her tracks at the top of the stairs. She was instantly frozen in place and in time. She no longer was a mother; she was her previous self, small and vulnerable again. Kay started to shake uncontrollably and felt an overwhelming urge to sit down. So that is exactly what she did. She sat, cross-legged at the top of the stairs. The cooks and maids thought she was nuts. Dr. Cain must have missed her presence because it wasn't long before he went to see what was taking her so long. She was only putting her daughter to bed. Tara was a bit of chitchat, but it was bedtime. Kay met his gaze as he suddenly appeared at the foot of the stairs. He looked like he had seen a ghost. His jaw dropped open when he saw Kay. She was dumb struck. For once in her life, she could not speak. Dr. Cain just stared at her.

Suddenly, from nowhere there was a strange amber glow. Almost like a mist in the air. It was calming and Kay realized she had just been sitting on the stairs sobbing uncontrollably. Her cotton blouse was soaked through to her skin. She had mascara and eyeliner running down her chin and her eyes were already red and swollen. Kay stood bolt upright immediately and began smoothing down the front of her wrinkled slacks.

Dr. Cain spoke first. Kay, my Dear, are you all right? You were crying. Is Tara all right? What, in the hell is going on with you; you're starting to scare me, Kay. First you won't discuss your lucid dream, then you and Tara disappear into the woods for hours on end and now I find you sitting on the top landing sobbing to break your heart. I think I deserve some sort of an explanation, don't I?" He finished, finally taking a breath as his face was starting to turn purple.

Kay heard her own words before she thought them. She was truly amazed to hear her own voice. "Yes, Dr. Cain, by all means. You do deserve an explanation. Please, let's go get that coffee now, shall we?" Kay said with a flourish of her hand and out to the kitchen she marched.

When Kay got to her kitchen destination, she stopped abruptly and sat at the small table the cooks used for their breaks. She found a pack of cigarettes; one of the cooks must have left behind. Kay took out a cigarette and with shaking fingers she lit a match and drew in deeply on that first puff. Immediately, she snapped fully back to reality and to the business at hand. She realized where she was and why she was here. It was like an epiphany; Kay knew what she had to do. She had been in a fog ever since her last trip to Dreamland, when she was 7 years old, like Tara. Kay had been so totally terrified of Dreamland that the mere mention of it threw her into a panic attack. The panic attacks had been gone for years, but lately they were back. There was something in her head and heart that told her she was about to embark on a well travelled and ill remembered, familiar journey. No wonder she had been having the attacks again. She was totally consumed by Tara's trips to Dreamland, of all places. The word scared the hell out of her. Now, Kay had to think and fast. She had promised Dr. Cain an explanation, now she had to come up with one.

"Kay, my God, you had me scared to death. You didn't even look like yourself. You were smaller somehow and younger, much younger." Dr. Cain finally stopped to take a breath.

Kay leapt at this opportunity to change the subject, so she blurted out "I'll get the coffee." And with that Kay was on her feet brewing coffee.

"Now, it's like you're energized. That picnic really must have done something to you. Even Tara couldn't wait to get to bed." Dr. Cain was rambling now and not really asking any direct questions.

Kay was thinking the whole time that she was making the coffee. She had almost fully formulated her plan on how to "confide" in Dr. Cain without really telling him anything. Too soon, the coffee was ready, and Kay was up, ready or not. "Well," she began, "we had a wonderful time at the picnic, and it just made me miss Drew and my mother even more. I guess I got a little sentimental when Tara asked me how come I don't miss my mother. It hit me that she thinks that I don't miss Mother just because I'm terrified of the Dreams and of Dreamland." Kay trailed off.

Dr. Cain looking knowingly into Kay's eyes and smiled. "Of course, at her age she would think that your fear of her dreams and Dreamland means that you don't miss her grandmother anymore. It does make perfect sense. That's probably why she sees your mother in her dreams all the time. All you have to do is keep talking about your mother, but in a positive way, talk about good things not any painful memories." Dr. Cain was beaming with pride at his newest discovery.

He had unraveled the nightmare mystery. Now, Kay knew what her mother had meant when she said Kay would have to help on Earth to protect Tara from all forces. This was the wrong direction that I was supposed to point him in.

"First thing in the morning, Kay we will get Tara up and immediately ask her to recall her dream from tonight. I'm sorry Kay but we have to cut this short I have so much to prepare for tomorrow. Good night, Dear, sleep well." Dr. Cain mumbled over his left shoulder as he exited the kitchen for his own wing.

Kay was stunned. How had she done that, and why had it been so easy. She wondered if those Throgs were out and about on Earth, helping her along. As amazed as she was with herself and her newfound abilities, she was feeling the strain. Kay stood up, stretched and tidied up the kitchen, before heading for her warm feather bed. As she entered her bedroom, she knew instinctively that someone had been in her room, and something was in the wrong place. Kay was a little anal when it came to the order of things. Obsessive-compulsive behavior was one term that sprung to her mind. She sat on the bed and looked around the room slowly. Her eyes finally settled on her nightstand. Her diary had been moved. She had left strict instructions for no maids or staff to enter her room. How could this have happened? Was it staff or was it the "good Doctor"? Kay knew then that her instincts had proven to be good earlier when she had decided to write in her old secret language. She giggled to herself; it was almost like being 7 again. Kay put her diary back on the nightstand and started getting ready for bed. Tara's words were in her head as she lay still under her covers and closed her eyes. Then Kay started to think about the safe room in Dreamland and meeting Tara there. As Kay drifted, she knew she'd be in Dreamland any second.

Chapter 13

Suddenly, there she was in the open doorway of the safe room in Dreamland. Her mother and daughter were already there, waiting. They both looked a little apprehensive as they watched her cross the room to where they stood. Kay gingerly stepped between the children, playing on the floor and crossed to meet her family. Kay smiled, tentatively, and said "Hey! I made it."

"Mommy! I knew you'd make it! Could you hear me talking to you in my head?" Tara was so excited that Kay had arrived as planned.

"I could feel your thoughts and they guided me through." Kay responded, pre-occupied.

"Ok, girls, we have a lot of work to do tonight and not very much time." Elizabeth commanded. "First, we have to meet with the Throgs. They have been working tirelessly on finding the weakness. They are waiting for us in a secret place hidden in the walls of the Great Hall. Follow me, we have no time to waste," Elizabeth finished out of breath.

Elizabeth led the way back out of the safe room into the dank, darkened hallway. Kay could hear the same faint noises as they made their way along the path. Tara looked to be watching something amusing and Elizabeth plunged on.

As the trio deftly picked their way along the, almost invisible, path there seemed to be a faint golden glow. Almost like a mist.

Kay froze. This was exactly like the incident just prior to her going head-to-head with Dr. Cain. It had been her first baby step into the 'plan' as an active participant. Until the first 'mist' she had only been a passive observer to her entire life. Now, not only was she in Dreamland, on purpose, but she was in what could arguably be, the most destiny changing trio of the history of the universe. She slowly started to shake it off. As she did, Tara shrieked" Look Mommy, a Squiggly!"

"Tara, honey! Are you alright!" Elizabeth whispered in such a sharp tone that it almost sounded like a screech. But everyone knew Elizabeth was the calming one. She didn't scream, screech or shriek. The fear in Elizabeth's eyes was like a sub-zero wind chill in your bones. Kay shivered at the sight of her mother's eyes. Tara just looked up at the two women and giggled.

"Can't you see them, guys?" Tara continued, unabated.

"They're like little red and orange glowing worms. They change colours when they move around and the faster, they move the brighter they glow. They live in the middle, Mommy. Don't you remember?" Tara asked her mother in surprise. "I know that you know them because they told me so. Mommy, you've got to remember, from when you were me." Tara finished, flushed in her face from the excitement of her own realization. "Mommy! I know now, I'm you because they were mean to you when you were you. So then they had to wait for me to come and me and Gram would make you not afraid." Tara was really on a roll now.

"I know who the 'little one' really is now Mommy and we can do it now, together. Remember the power of three." Tara stopped short. She looked from her mother to her grandmother and the look of terror grew with each blink of her innocent eyes. "We have to go, NOW!" Tara said, as her adult alter ego, Kay remembered from Tara's own room, with the red glow. That was Tara and the golden mist must be her Mother. Together they were just like the worms and Grandma was the glowing part. She was everywhere and always thought she went nowhere. No time to think. Tara's mind was reeling.

Elizabeth grabbed Tara's hand and then took Kay's hand in hers. Now they had to use their God given power of three. They had a universe to protect. Elizabeth was like an Olympic runner and Kay and Tara were like streamers in her wake. They wound lower and deeper into Dreamland. They needed to be at the base of operations. It is always in the basement. So, lower and lower they seemed to descend. The air was somehow fresher. The temperature increased and there was an eerie glow about everything.

Together they could face anything and that is exactly what they had ahead of them. Everything and anything that was imaginable was here in Dreamland, to be faced. After all that was the whole nature and purpose of Dreamland, for the imagination. It was the only safe place to come and dream. Every dream has already been dreamt, or has it? Dreamland was the other half. It had to exist in order for the Earth to exist. It was the frick to Earth's frack. The 'plan' had to work, it was all they had.

Finally, as they rounded the last corner into the vortex of Dreamland, Kay was awestruck. She had never imagined anything this intricate. The detail in the core of Dreamland was astounding. Tara stopped short and just stared. "It's beautiful, isn't it, Mommy. Aren't you glad we came here?" Tara whispered.

Kay looked down into her daughters' eyes and saw a wisdom beyond her years. "Tara, my little one, you and your grandmother were right all this time. We were meant to be here." Kays' voice trailed off.

"Never mind, now, my two little ones, we have no time to waste." Elizabeth said, trying to get them to focus on the issue at hand.

As the three women stood on the last leg of the path into the Great Hall, within the core of Dreamland, they all came to one realization. They were definitely there for a reason.

The walls seemed to vibrate with hidden inner life. There was that familiar red glow all around the outer walls. There was an amber mist swirling lazily around the ceiling and floor. The calm in the Great Hall was palpable. The power of three! Tara had the vision, in more ways than one. Kay had the feeling complimented by acute hearing and Elizabeth exuded calm. Nothing appeared to move but there was the unmistakable feel of perpetual motion. The 'Squigglies' Tara had described seemed to flicker up and down the outside walls with the combined effect of red glow, amber mist and pulsating calm. The entire hall took on a renewed red orange misty smouldering warmth.

The Throgs were off the Great Hall in the east tunnel. Elizabeth led Tara and Kay around the outer rim of the path surrounding the Great Hall. As they made their way to the entrance of the east tunnel, Kay noticed that the Great Hall seemed to go up forever. Just as she was about to mention it Tara was ripped from her grasp. Elizabeth froze as Kay screamed "Tara!! Where are you?"

"Did you see anything, Kay?" Elizabeth asked in an urgent whisper.

"Nothing. I can hear scuttling sounds. It seems like it's coming from inside the wall." Kay answered, in a breathless panic. "Mother, where is she?" Kay begged her.

"I'm afraid that the Throgs are not the only ones that know of our presence. She is safe inside the walls now, hopefully following the Squigglies." Elizabeth finished tentatively.

"What do you mean, inside the wall. Mother, even in Dreamland that is impossible." Kay was getting angry now.

"Nothing is impossible Kay, especially in Dreamland. You must be open to everything. She is safe, I can feel it. She must go with the Squigglies to find her true destiny. They will show her the way back. We must hurry, now. The Throgs will help us find her." Elizabeth was on the move again, faster now. They quickly followed the path to the East Tunnel and to the Throgs. Kay could only pray that her mother was right and that Tara was safe, wherever she was.

Near the entrance to the East Tunnel there appeared to be a huge, bejewelled panel off to one side. As they approached the tunnel entrance this panel began to glow. The same red glow was emanating from around the door just like in Tara's room. Then the amber mist started to gather, only this time it too was surrounding the panel. Then there was the eeriest combination of light, colour and energy Kay had ever seen. She quickly glanced at her mother's face to gauge her level of knowledge about this panel. To Kay's shock her mother looked even more surprised than Kay did. The whole panel began to pulse with life and red and orange squiggly things seemed to be racing back and forth across the panel. Kay was still wrestling with the depth of meaning this all had for her when the panel gratingly slid to one side. There stood Tara in an amazing flash of lights. The tunnel of light behind Tara seemed to go on for eternity and never dim or flicker. It was the most beautiful light Kay or Elizabeth had ever seen. Tara stood like a miniature angel in the heavenly glowing light as she beckoned for her mother and grandmother to join her. Elizabeth and Kay joined hands and tentatively stepped into the light and Tara's outstretched hands.

They seemed to float effortlessly across the threshold of the wall panel. Tara was like a silvery white fairy child enshrined in this tunnel of white glowing mist. It was surreal, like a white campfire. The white changed shades like a log on fire, in flickering waves.

Tara stood, like a giant, in her element. Kay finally realized, in her core, what her family's destiny really was, and she wasn't sure she really liked it.

The next thing Kay knew it was morning. Was Tara all right? Did any of this really happen or was it only a dream? Kay shuddered at the thought it may be real and then harder when she thought it might be only a dream. She bolted from her room in a desperate search for her innocent daughter. As she rounded the corner, she ran smack into Dr. Cain. He was heading for the back of the house, and she thought he looked a little dazed. Kay had almost knocked his coffee out of his hand, and he didn't even say good morning. Kay knew the look; he was definitely a man on a mission.

As she was catching her breath, Tara appeared. "Mommy! Wasn't that cool last night? Mommy?" Tara was so excited, and Kay just froze. "Yes, dear." was all Kay could say.

After a few silent seconds Kay rebounded and said, more forcefully now "Breakfast? I'm starving. Let's go Tara." Kay took Tara by her little hand and was comforted that they had made it back safely, with memories intact. They had a great deal of transcribing to do. One good thing was that Dr. Cain was gone to the back lab and would probably be gone for the rest of the day. Kay knew he was up to something, but she had her own plan for the day. She and Tara could spend the whole day discussing and transcribing all the details and their feelings about all of this. Kay knew that this was an experience she and Tara could share with generations of future Dreamland explorers.

Chapter 14

Dr. Cain tossed and turned. Finally abandoning his bed for the night, he went to his computer lab. He could hardly wait to do his research on his little patient's fixation on her grandmother. This was a new psychological slant on the mother daughter syndrome. This was a totally different twist on an age old and accepted theory of mother daughter relationships.

It was Grandmother and Granddaughter. This was unique, new and, best of all, it was his, all his. Unbeknownst to the 'good doctor', the evil forces of Dreamland had already begun their work. It was the Nightmare Fairies. They had come to visit and fill Dr. Cain's head with all sorts of impossible discoveries. The first of which was the thought that we, mere mortals, could even conceive of viewing the unconscious wanderings of a free soul, visiting Dreamland. How could an educated man such as the 'good doctor' really believe he was capable of such a major discovery? The Nightmare Fairies, that's who. They could convince anyone of anything. That was the power they possessed as fairies.

Too bad for Dr. Cain, he had no idea what was really happening, to him or in Dreamland. The Nightmare Fairies were trying to turn his inner evil into a more powerful force that his innate goodness. This was one of their specialties.

As the night wore on, Dr. Cain sat at his computer tirelessly poring over his formulas and charts. He felt that he was on the very brink of the most important discovery of his career.

He was definitely in the zone. He labored over his calculations well into the early morning hours. The sun was just breaking its way up into the fresh morning sky. As it slowly rose Dr. Cain came to a major realization. He had developed a computer program that would allow him a glimpse into Tara's head and her dreams. It had all been so simple when it finally came to him. It was like a vision; it was so simple.

Dr. Cain sprang to his feet and went straight to the window, overlooking the valley. Could this, his Sleep Centre, be the real place that Seth had lived in the 1700's or 1800's? Dr. Cain decided right then and there that he had to cancel anything with Tara or Kay this whole day. He had to review his research of this location for the Sleep Centre. He had transcribed his work onto laser discs as he completed it so he could have easy access to it here at the centre. Today was the first day of the rest of his career and he could ill afford any mindless distractions. He could hear, in his head, a tiny voice warning him that he was starting to sound like the classic mad scientist. He could not remember the last time he had felt the rush of his insatiable thirst for knowledge.

For the first time since he had founded the Sleep Centre, he had completely forgotten Tara and her dreams. After all, he and Ruthie had founded this Centre with a child like Tara in mind. They had no idea at that time Tara even existed. Dr. Cain had only met her a year and a half ago. He had been giving a seminar at a local Hotel for charity and Mr. & Mrs. Prescott had come to listen. They even invited him, to lunch the next day, to meet their daughter, Tara. The first time Dr. Cain laid eyes on Tara he knew she was special. He was only, now, beginning to realize just how special Tara really was.

He couldn't believe his good fortune at his potential discovery. He was all about the recognition, for Ruthie, he kept telling himself. He had to do it for Ruthie. His one and only love. His best friend, his confidante, his soul mate. She would guide him, through this; he knew that in his soul. She was always with him, even since she passed. Never more than a blink away. In order to totally focus on this new and intriguing perspective on his sleep research he had to keep distractions to a minimum. That would mean making thoughts of Ruthie, Tara and Kay go away for the day. Today he had to be 100% focused on his research and nothing could be permitted to deter him from his plan.

He headed for his private bathroom and only emerged a full thirty minutes later. Neatly dressed, showered and shaved Dr. Cain headed straight for the back of the lab, where all the early research was stored. He was as excited as a small child on their Birthday. There was dust everywhere. Dr. Cain had not been in this wing in several years now and had almost forgotten how massive his research collection was. He headed for the light switch and tried not to breathe too deeply, as the stench of mildewed paper and leather was too pungent to endure in large doses. The odour was as tangible as the bright fluorescent ceiling lights that were now softly buzzing to life. All together it was, to Dr. Cain, an amazing sight. Rows and rows of shelves that stood like little soldiers in neat little aisles.

They were meticulously described on the exteriors of the file containers. Some were old cardboard file boxes and others were miniature metal file cabinets, but they all were full to overflowing with the evidence of a very distinguished career in clinical scientific research.

Dr. Cain was immediately relieved he had left a comfortable overstuffed armchair back here and grateful he had thought to bring his coffee. He sat slowly in his favourite old chair and sighed heavily as he looked around this warehouse sized, vault like library of his life's work. This was a beautiful place; he thought to himself, I have a great deal to be thankful for and proud of. There seemed to be some inner struggle he felt he was going through, today. Like he was struggling with the forces of evil. He shook his head and decided that the best use of his day would be to research this property, in detail and fast. His youthful sense of urgency had returned, and he knew that his late wife would have been proud of him right now. Why was he thinking of Ruthie all of a sudden? He hadn't thought about his wife in all the months since he had met Tara and her parents at the dream seminar. This was definitely a sign of something, he knew that much at least.

When he caught his breath, Dr. Cain began booting up the old computer he kept here, for just such an occasion. He scanned through his real estate research, from when he and his wife Ruth had purchased this place. Originally, this was their little refuge from the world. They came here to relax, read, write, eat, sleep, dream and whatever else they wanted to do, in peace. He had been hounded for his controversial research on the human brain in development from a baby, through adolescence and finally into adulthood. The research was ingenious, groundbreaking and widely revered by his colleagues but damned by the public. It was the most inspired and unpopular research discovery of all scientific history. It was banned from the scientific journals and his laboratory procedures were denounced as evil madness, maybe even mad scientist tactics.

No one was prepared to believe the results of his own non-invasive, research procedures for seeing brain waves on a computerized graph. These could be used in compiling the necessary research data to complete his process. Brain waves of all things! Now, or at least soon, he could dust off his invention and graph Tara's dreams. Then he could tie all the ends together and solve this intricate puzzle of a girl. Right now, he had to focus on the current puzzle piece, the Sleep Centre location. Ruthie had always said she could feel things here. She was the sensitive one of their union. Man, he really missed her right now. He had always felt closest to her here; even the memories linger in the air, in our little hideaway library. She had always called this room that name. The 'hideaway library' had always been its official nickname and even the smell was comforting now. This research project would go more quickly, now that Ruthie was there to help him, he could feel her presence. The weight of this project immediately lessened by half.

The day and night seemed to pass very quickly with the necessary files he needed practically leaping into his open hand. By late afternoon of what Dr. Cain thought was day two in the attic, Dr. Cain's stomach began to grumble.

He only then realized that he hadn't eaten since dinner last night. He hadn't eaten the whole day before worrying about Tara and Kay on their picnic, and he was starving. As he stood up to stretch, he could feel his age. The dampness had settled deep in his bones. He must remember that tomorrow to dress more warmly or bring a heater.

Dr. Cain gathered up all of his documents and discs to take to his room with him. He needed everything locked up with him at night. Especially with them hopping in and out of some crazy dream called Dreamland. The entire idea of a collective dream sequence with two or more participants was the next step in his old research and he felt that he needed to continue on with this particular part of the old research. The logical next step was to figure out what was really in their dreams? Could he really see their thoughts and dreams? Only time would tell, what was to be. Dr. Cain realized that he had only been cautiously optimistic all of his life and now it was time to be truly optimistic and finally believe in his own abilities. Ruthie would be so proud of him, he thought to himself, as he settled in to read some of his research until his company rose for the day. He was tired but excited at this new perspective on his research. He felt revived and ready to explore all the new possibilities of his Sleep Centre and its history. He truly believed that there was a connection between this property and Tara's dreams. Now, he had to figure out what that connection was, and he had to do it quickly before Tara and Kay left the Centre. He somehow knew that he didn't have a great deal of time to find out what he needed. Soon, Kay would start to ask what he was doing. He just had to make sure that this new direction of his plan didn't interfere with his patient and her mother, after all they were the critical piece of this puzzle, that much he already knew.

Suddenly, he felt that evil mad scientist feeling wash over him again. This feeling was similar to the one that had initially engulfed him when he first realized his attic library was actually a vault.

Just like in the attic book vault, when he realized that he had installed magnetic inner walls in that room. The room was soundproof but had an inner sprinkler system in case of fire and a set of combination locks on the door. Now it really was a vault. It even had that musty old book smell.

Dr. Cain had been working on a computer program to view Tara's dreams and it was not going well. He had spent days trying to perfect the program and he was rapidly running out of time. He knew that once Tara left the Sleep Centre, he would no longer have his "guinea pig" to work out his program on. Tara spoke of Dreamland like it was a real place people could visit in their dreams, but he had never heard of such a thing, so he wanted to keep her at the Centre as long as possible. This would give him more time to perfect his video-brain wave program. This would enable him to actually see where Tara was in her Dreams. Zorlak could not afford for this to happen, especially now when Dreamland and the whole world was at stake. Dr. Cain was only getting in the way.

Chapter 15

After a very short clean up Dr. Cain headed for the kitchen to see what was for dinner. When he walked in Kay and Tara were sitting at the table whispering conspiratorially. When he entered, they immediately stopped and looked up at him. In perfect unison they sang" Long Time, No See" and then Kay on her own "We were beginning to worry about you. We thought you had retreated to your attic hideout for good."

"Well, ladies it is nice to be missed. But I've been very busy doing research for our program here the past day or so. I've been digging into the history of this house and the grounds and area around it. I think that this house has a history and that it might be very interesting." Dr. Cain stopped breathlessly.

It hit Kay then, like a slap in the face, he had no idea how long he had been gone. He thought this was still the first morning, when it really was the next evening. Day one was the picnic, all day. Everybody worried about the 'Woman Folk'. It was a very long day for some and a very short day for a mother and daughter spending the day together doing Dreamland research. Somehow, the 'good doctor' had lost a full day. He seemed to be expecting breakfast rather than dinner. It had been one long day for the 'good doctor' and two full days and one night for the Dreamland duo. They were looking forward to night three in Dreamland, together. Yet Dr. Cain hadn't even been to sleep yet. Not a wink since the morning of the picnic.

"After dinner we can hear all about it by the fire, then? "Kay asked off hand. "Tara and I are starving. Let's eat!" she stood with a flourish of her hand and began warming up the delicious dinner the cooks had left for them.

Kay had left strict instructions with them that if the doctor needed either of them to let Kay know right away. They had enjoyed their day uninterruptedly. Kay and Tara were busy discussing the previous nights' events in Dreamland and what they all meant. There seemed to be so many important messages they had received there, both of them had taken the entire day just to begin to digest it.

No one was really listening as Dr. Cain updated Tara and Kay on the previous evenings research results.

They were only too grateful for Dr. Cain's newfound interest in researching the Sleep Centre site. If anything, they felt this could be just the distraction they had been looking for all along.

Dr. Cain was equally content with the results of what he had thought was one day. He had amassed a great deal of material to reread this evening in his room. They could all sit by the fire in the study, and he could tell them how exciting a turn his research had most recently taken.

The evening passed very quickly with Dr. Cain reciting his day's activities and the new theory he had. He was talking about the Sleep Centre itself and how it all meant something. Then he moved onto the topic of his computerized dream snooper program and its new application.

Before long, Kay made a plea of exhaustion and she and Tara went off to bed leaving Dr. Cain with his own thoughts. His head seemed so muddled with all of the new information he had gathered. He needed some sleep himself. He was exhausted and becoming more so by the moment. As he rose to leave the study, he thought he could hear a small child crying. He went to Tara's room, and she wasn't crying she was singing. He went back towards the study and the noise grew louder. He flung open the door to the study hoping to catch whoever it was. The crying had stopped so abruptly that it startled Dr. Cain. He just stood there with his mouth and the door wide open. There was nothing in the study that he could see. There was a subtle breeze when he had opened the door, but he figured that was from the way he had opened it. Now he knew he had reached the breaking point in his exhaustion. He was starting to hallucinate now. It definitely was time for some hard-earned rest. Dr. Cain headed for his room with nothing on his mind but sleep.

Kay had gone straight to her own room after tucking Tara in. Tara had been sweetly singing her favourite bedtime lullaby. Kay was satisfied they had succeeded in recording both trips to Dreamland together, in their own language codes of course, and now they were on their way back to Dreamland for their third night in a row. Kay wondered if they would have to start all over again or could they just pick up where they had left off. She had only been there a few times, but she did think that they would be able to start right where they had left off. Oh well, she thought, she would know soon enough. She cuddled into her feather bed, pulled the covers up to her chin and lazily drifted off to Dreamland. She thought only of her daughter and her mother and soon she was with them in the core of Dreamland. All three together again.

Dr. Cain had not had as good luck as Kay had in falling asleep. He was still tossing and turning, long after the rest of the house was silent with sleep. He finally got out of bed and went back into the study. He couldn't stop thinking about the child crying he thought he had heard. It was gnawing at him now. He looked all over the study now and could find no evidence of anyone, let alone a child.

Convinced he had been hallucinating, he returned to his bed with a glass of warm milk. By the time the milk was gone so was Dr. Cain. He finally fell asleep.

Somehow, Dr. Cain knew he was asleep and dreaming, but he appeared more alert than he ever had been in a dream before. It was just like being awake but in a dream. That was it, the key to the dream state and how to gather more information on it. Tara must be awake in her dreams. That would explain why she thinks it's real. She is convinced that she really saw her grandmother and even spoke to her. Dr. Cain relaxed just enough to forget to be awake and really drifted off. He slept soundly the rest of the night and when he woke the next morning, he was grateful for the rest. One more day in the attic should unearth the balance of the research Dr. Cain needed to complete this new phase of his master plan. There he was again playing the mad scientist. Oh well, at least today he wasn't the mad evil scientist he had been accused of so many times. He was now starting to believe that this new phase would also lend credibility to his old research on brain waves. He headed straight for the kitchen as soon as he was showered and dressed. He ate his breakfast hastily and left a note for Kay and Tara. All the note said was "One more day in the attic and then I truly can help Tara," signed Dr. Cain.

He refilled his coffee carafe and grabbed his mug off the counter, turned and left the main part of the house/centre for another full day.

As he entered his attic library, he noticed a different smell in the room. It smelled like Ruthie's perfume she had always worn. He settled in to reconstruct the history of this property. He began at the turn of the 19th century, the 1800's. This had always been the era that Dr. Cain had been especially intrigued by. This was pre-Civil War times of huge prosperity and sprawling mansions. The slave trade was still alive and well in this part of the South. Tara's descendants dated back to the battle of Bull Run. That one was almost on the very spot of the Sleep Centre grounds. That was what made this property perfect for his research and rehabilitation Sleep Centre. This had been a turn of the century mansion where history abounded. Dr. Cain had a brief flash of how much knowledge was within these walls. Then, immediately he began thinking of the personal recognition and the money. He was already beginning to lose focus of the real purpose of this research and being swayed by the pervasive evil of the Nightmare Fairies. He was determined to prove his scientific ability to the real world, himself and the entire scientific community. He was becoming consumed by the thirst for validation and acceptance. Dr. Cain was only realizing that he needed this now, more than anything. If he could die with his research exonerated of anything evil or undesirable and his scientific reputation restored. He needed to make Ruthie proud one last time and he wasn't getting any younger. She had followed him here from the big city, in shame and exile. He had to prove to her that he was not a loser but an intelligent, honourable man.

He had never, knowingly hurt anyone, ever. He needed vindication and he needed it soon. He could feel his health failing. He finally understood what that expression meant. He knew in his heart and soul that he was weakening and would soon become ill more often and more severely until he died of something. He knew he only needed the last hundred and fifty years or so.

He sat at his keyboard and began scrolling back to 1850, and then he realized it would be easier to just write down what he already knew about Tara and just work backwards until it made sense. He knew that idea came from Ruthie. She always had a backwards approach to research. She always wanted to start from today and go backwards. All other researchers go back as far as they think they need to and build forward. He started with their names, dates of birth, relationships and piece of the puzzle:

Child: Tara Serenity Prescott DOB: January 1, 2001, The Dreamer

Mother: Katherine Elizabeth Prescott AKA: Kay DOB: January 1, 1964, The Helper (Nee: Beauregarde)

Father: Andrew Patrick Prescott AKA: Drew DOB: September 9, 1959, The Stabilizer

Kay's Mother: Elizabeth Ruth Beauregarde DOB: January 7, 1924, The Calming One (Nee: Johnstone)

Kay's Father: Jacob Patrick Beauregarde DOB: October 10, 1920, Bull Run Descendent

(His Great Grandfather Colonel Jacob Elijah Beauregarde was at the Battle of Bull Run)

Dr. Cain stopped right there. This was huge, he had found a connection between the Sleep Centre property and Tara. Her Grandfather had been a Bull Run descendent. Her Great, Great Grandfather was the one and only Colonel Jacob Beauregarde from the actual Battle of Bull Run. That felt too good to be true. The Nightmare Fairies were hard at work today in the attic. They were having some good-natured fun with the 'good doctor'. They had him convinced, hastily that this was the one and only connection, but they knew there were other connections. They were the ones that had made Dr. Cain bring Tara and Kay here in the first place. There was, in this old mansion, one of the only direct tunnels to Dreamland, but the Nightmare Fairies weren't about to tell Dr. Cain that part. The rest of the tunnels were all destroyed by the civil unrest that had haunted the south. There were many connections to Tara in the rooms of this old house. Her appearance had been predicted for centuries, prior to her arrival, but Dr. Cain was never going to know all of the connections. The Nightmare Fairies would see to that, no doubt. Their mission was to distract Dr. Cain and to promote his innate evil side. They were allowing him to discover just enough to pique his interest but not enough to let him truly figure out Tara's true connection to Dreamland. Even the Nightmare Fairies, which were mostly evil, didn't want to witness the end of Dreamland. They were sent by Zorlak himself and they really wanted to make him happy. Over the years the relationship between them and their fearless leader had been a little strained, to say the least. No resident of Dreamland wanted to see it fall. That would mean the end of all civilization on earth too. That would be the end of everything, and no one wanted that outcome.

At least there was still a common goal in Dreamland, even though one had ceased to exist on earth centuries ago. The Nightmare Fairies were really having fun with Dr. Cain. He was a more intelligent person than they were used to dealing with. He was well read, well educated and very intuitive. He was a bit more of a challenge, but they didn't mind, they were enjoying themselves.

This babysitting job was the easiest job they had taken on lately. It was almost fun not to hurt people. They could be tolerable to the point of not nasty. No Nightmare Fairy had ever been accused of being nice.

Meanwhile, Dr. Cain was busily piecing together the history of this house and land. There had never been a slave bought, sold, or hired at this estate. This had always been a humane facility even when it was an estate in the south during slavery. There were never any slaves under any roof on this entire property. The more in-depth Dr. Cain's research became the more he knew that there were good, positive forces at work in the Centre. What he found was of no surprise to him. Colonel Jacob Beauregarde was a hero at Bull Run. He had a wonderfully happy family, which included many brothers and sisters, aunts and uncles, not to mention his loving wife Annabella and their son Seth. Colonel Jacob

Beauregarde wrote intriguing recollections of battles he had fought and historical essays about Atlanta and life there in the 1800's.

Dr. Cain could not believe his eyes as he gradually found out enough to move on with. He knew that if he continued on this vein, he could unravel the entire puzzle. At the same time Dr. Cain also knew that time was the one thing he did not have, right now.

He had to complete enough so that he had a solid background from which to start his evaluation of Tara. He had always been able to gather the right amount of information with which to begin or continue his research. His tactics were not always the most widely accepted methods. Most other research scientists preferred to take as much time as necessary to gather all the pertinent information prior to doing any test trials or publishing results. Dr. Cain seemed to gather just enough data to get through but on closer inspection there were always crucial details he had overlooked. This had always been his downfall, although he never saw it that way. His way was the best way, as far as he was concerned.

Maybe that was why Dr. Cain had been the scientist selected to research these new phenomena. He had always been able to resist the forces of evil in the scientific community. It wouldn't be too hard for him to get involved with the darker side of science. He, Dr. Cain, now knew the solution to the puzzle that was Tara. Was there really such a place as Dreamland, no, Dr. Cain was not yet prepared to believe that it existed.

He didn't have the time or the patience to dig through any more old data. Time was of the essence, Kay and Tara had to be monitored and soon. Dr. Cain felt an overwhelming urge to run and find Tara and Kay. He needed to speak to Kay and try to find out what she knew about her ancestors.

This would be the single largest scientific breakthrough of all time and Dr. Cain felt free to be proud of his accomplishments. He would do this no matter what tactics he had to employ; no holds barred. This potential discovery was too important to risk anything to chance. He needed for this plan, to use Tara's dreams to validate his early research, to work.

When Dr. Cain decided he was finished for the day he returned to the kitchen to find out how suspicious his behaviour had seemed to his guests. He was unconcerned at their reaction as it was only another piece of this unfolding puzzle. He knew that what he was doing was extremely important to the welfare of the earth and its entire realm, whatever that entailed. He just couldn't figure out why he felt such life and death urgency in his research.

He was quite pleased to see Kay and Tara sitting at the dinner table waiting for him, when he entered the kitchen. "Good evening, ladies." Dr. Cain almost bellowed.

"Good evening, doctor." They replied in unison.

"What have you two been up to today, anything interesting?" Dr. Cain continued.

"We've been exploring the grounds and the gardens all day." Kay lied with a smile.

"Yeah, what pretty flowers there are in the gardens? Dr. Cain, who looks after them all the time when you're not here?" Tara asked innocently.

"Oh, dear, I have a gardener who looks after that now that Mrs. Cain is gone." Dr. Cain responded distractedly.

"Oh, Dr. Cain, I'm sorry about your wife. How long has it been since she passed?" Kay asked shyly.

"Well, it has been just over seven years. She died on New Year's Eve, seven years ago.," he answered.

"That's just before I was born, Dr. Cain did you know that?" Tara asked.

"I hadn't realized that dear. I guess you may have crossed paths that night." Dr. Cain muttered.

Kay spoke next. "Tara, honey I think we should go to bed early tonight and let Dr. Cain rest. He seems very tired from all that time in the attic."

Dr. Cain sat up with a start. "I must apologize for my neglectful behavior these past two days. I have been on the brink of a new discovery, and it tends to absorb all of my attention. Tomorrow will be different. It is well past time for us to commence our assessment of Tara." He paused and continued "Let's all get a good night's sleep and get started right after breakfast in the morning?" he asked.

"Great idea, doctor. Come on Tara; let's go read a bedtime story. Good night, Dr. Cain." Kay finished as she stood up, took Tara's hand and headed for her daughter's room.

Dr. Cain sat quietly for a long moment and then got a glass of warm milk and headed for his own room. He did not toss or turn tonight; he was too worn out from analyzing everything all day.

He had to shake it off. This was two days in a row that he had escaped from his responsibility to Kay and Tara. He was starting to worry, now. No wonder Ruthie was around constantly. Maybe he really was turning into the evil mad scientist his wife had always warned him about becoming. Dr. Cain just realized that he had been gone for two full days and two full nights. He had discovered an enormous amount of information about Tara and Kay and their families.

It seemed to Dr. Cain that these women, both young and not so young, were unique in more than one way. They were definitely connected to the Sleep Centre property. There was no doubt in Dr. Cain's mind now. He knew that this centre had a major piece in the history of Kay and Tara's family. He had traced it back to Bull Run; the entire family history was there. He had yet to investigate Andrew's family, but they also showed promise. It was a fertile time with money and culture galore. This part of the South was the most prestigious neighborhood in Atlanta. Only the richest of the rich and the most famous of the famous could afford to live here. The old Stone Cliff Manor, now known as the Sleep Centre, was the cornerstone of Atlanta high society. The Beauregarde's would never have condoned anything less than equal treatment in all aspects of human life. They were much revered in their day and still talked about in the upper echelons of high society even today. Ruthie used to love the effect that Stone Cliff Manor had on her reputation in the community.

Dr. Cain always could feel the good karma that existed here. He had always felt safe and warm within these hallowed walls. The good energy was pervasive and intoxicating. That was why he and his Ruthie selected this property, for the comfort and warmth it had given them immediately and also for years later.

Chapter 16

As soon as they knew Dr. Cain had retreated to his attic library, Kay and Tara headed for the study. They had a lot to do today, and they had to hurry. Although they had an entire day, free, ahead of them, they had a great deal to accomplish. Straight to the roll top desk, they trotted.

Tara sat in the huge red leather, overstuffed desk chair and put her little feet up on the desk. She said, in her best grown-up voice," Momma, here is where we can find out stuff. Trust me, the Throgs told me where to look. We can write everything from last night down and then we can snoop around for some new info." Tara finished with a satisfied sigh.

Kay was startled by the mature tone in her daughter's voice. She turned to see a very determined and mature look on Tara's little face. Could this still be her little girl, or would she ever be again? "Tara, honey, get your feet off of the desk. You might leave a mark. Get the pencils out of the drawer and I'll get the paper. We can start to write. Do you want to talk, and I'll write or the other way around?" Kay inquired of her young daughter.

"You can write faster than me, so I'll tell the story and you can write it down. Ok, Mommy?" Tara said, beaming at the thought of telling the story of Dreamland, to her mother. This was Tara's dream come true, and Grandma's too. Tara could hardly wait to tell her Momma the real-life story of Dreamland. "Hold on Momma, it might get bumpy." Tara said teasingly.

"When Gram and I were waiting for you, in the safe room, we started talking. We talked about how freaked out you were, growing up, about Dreamland. You actually became hysterical at the mere mention of Dreamland." Tara continued.

Kay knew then that her mother or her influence was not far away. If this wasn't a tag team match, then, nothing ever was. Kay was still mulling this thought over when the sound of her seven-year-old daughter's far too mature voice, snapped her back to reality. Her own daughter was actually reprimanding her for not paying close enough attention. This had to be Elizabeth's influence; Tara wasn't even old enough to think about discipline yet, at least in the sense of disciplining others. Kay's mind was reeling as she turned to focus on the task at hand.

"I have to tell you this story Momma, now, today, before we go back again tonight. There are important things you need to know." Tara said pleadingly.

The urgency in her daughters' voice made Kay shiver. She looked intently into Tara's eyes and shivered again. What she saw in her daughter's eyes astounded and intrigued her. Tara was wise beyond her years and had a matriarchal stance. Kay immediately understood that her daughter had spent a great deal of time with her grandmother in Dreamland and her wisdom of the ages showed, quite impressively too.

"Mother, are you listening or not?" Tara scolded.

Kay snapped to attention and really focused on her daughter. "Yes, dear, I am listening now. Sorry, I must have been daydreaming. Ok, go ahead I'm really ready now." Kay was trying to redeem herself with her daughter quickly so that they could get to work. They didn't have very much time.

When Tara started to speak, she was like a machine. She rattled on and on about the purpose of Dreamland and of the crucial time they were entering. The force of her daughter's rhetoric mesmerized Kay. Her voice was hypnotic and soothing. Kay could not believe her ears; her seven-year-old baby was wise beyond her years. Kay could not deny the warmth of the pride that was welling up inside her at the sight of her daughter, who was truly in her element.

"Mother! I need for you to be writing, as well as listening." Tara stated rather tersely.

Kay started to write every word that Tara spoke to her that afternoon. The funny thing was that she didn't remember anything she had written. By the end of the day Kay had written volumes of Tara thoughts, ideas and recollections. Kay could not believe how much she had written that day, and her hand wasn't even tired. They sat cuddled up by the roaring fire for hours that afternoon. Tara seemed to be exhausted by her ordeal. The story of Dreamland was only yet to be told, and they both knew it.

Tonight, would be the real test. They both were aware of the fact that Dreamland would unleash many secrets this night, never to be released again, ever. They analyzed and theorized on the sights, sounds and feelings they had experienced over their two visits together. It was nearly time for Dr. Cain to re-emerge, here it was after dinner and still no sign of him. Kay was beginning to get concerned about his new thirst for his research and she wondered idly about his real intentions with her and her daughter. A cold shiver coursed through her and left her with a heightened awareness of the good doctor's real plans for them.

Kay was reluctant to run into Dr. Cain this evening, so she got Tara ready for bed early and as soon as Tara fell asleep, Kay went straight to her room. As Kay pulled her down comforter up to her chin, she thought about the fact that she still could feel the chill from her shiver earlier. And she prayed for her safety and the safety of her loved ones as she quietly drifted off to Dreamland.

The next thing Kay knew she and her mother were hand in hand with Tara in her flowing white gown and still within the bright white tunnel. The first thought on Kay's mind was to question her mother on Dr. Cain and how much she had known about him when she let him bring them here, to the Sleep Centre. There was no real time to think about any of that, as they seemed to be floating behind Tara, further and further into the tunnel of light. Both Elizabeth and Kay just kept looking from Tara to each other in total confusion. Tara had such a grasp on them that they felt no fear and only confusion and wonder. Gradually, up ahead of them they could make out some shapes. Kay could hear tiny voices and laughter. She couldn't make out anything specific, but it looked like a group of really small children to Kay. Slowly Tara settled onto a platform with Elizabeth and Kay at either side. They seemed to be looking down at something but there was a thick fog surrounding it.

"Mother, Grandmother," Tara began "these are the Throgs and their pet Squigglies. They live in the very heart of Dreamland, and we cannot go there." As Tara continued both Elizabeth and Kay were mesmerized and amazed by the new tone in Tara's voice. She had a commanding presence, and they were definitely impressed by her ease in a leadership role.

"This is where all of them come to spend time with their friends. They all have to meet once a day to make sure there is nothing new that the rest of them need to know." Tara was speaking only to them, describing the scene before them. "They knew I was here, so they decided to come and get me. That was when I went through the wall, but you guys were okay, right?" Now Tara was starting to sound like herself again. "I learned how to speak to them without moving my lips. "Tara said excitedly. "That's really cool, especially because we all speak different words but we all have the same thoughts and feelings." Tara was really on a roll now.

She prattled on for several long moments about all the fun she had while she was with them and things she heard and saw, how terribly cool everything was. Meanwhile, Kay turned her attention to her mother and started asking questions. "Mother, exactly how long did you know about Dr. Cain and what are his true intentions for the uses of his discoveries. Will he help people or hurt them, and did he even care?" Kay was breathless.

Elizabeth took a deep breath, held it in for a moment and let it out with a huge sigh. The hair on the back of Kay's neck stood at attention. She had never seen her mother this humble. This couldn't be good. "Kay, my darling, I have known there would be a Dr. Cain, but I didn't ever know who it was. I have known that your first-born daughter would hold the key to the survival of Dreamland, for a very long time now. It would have been you, but the time wasn't right yet. It only recently occurred to me that it was actually the three of us, together. Remember, the power of three?" Elizabeth took another deep breath and continued. "Now, Dr. Cain is both villain and hero, Kay. We need him, for now, but if he gets out of control, we can handle it here in Dreamland. We three women have the power to save Dreamland and the world. We can worry about it later but right now we have bigger problems." Elizabeth and Tara and Kay were standing in a huddle.

Tara spoke next "We must learn a great deal tonight as time is getting short. We have much to learn and master in a very short time." There she was, the matriarch again, it was spooky, yet comforting.

"Mother, Grandmother, we need to move on through the mist to the other side. There are answers waiting there for us." Tara raised her left arm and the trio marched on. Tara could pick her way through even the densest of forested areas, clearing a path for her companions. As they cautiously made their way through this strange mist, Kay and Elizabeth were very aware of their surroundings. They could smell, hear and feel everything that was going on here. Learn as much as we can were the words ringing in Kay and Elizabeth's ears, over and over from Tara's lecture earlier. It was a strange walk, as the thorns seemed to get out of our way rather than the other way around. Tara led onward and they followed blindly through twists and turns even more abundant than the beautiful flowers, with their vibrant colors and breathtaking scents.

Eventually, Tara slowed her pace. They sat on a boulder and rested for a few minutes before Tara spoke. "Now, we will learn. We are entering Zenithia, the Inner Sanctum. This is a special and protected place where all of Dreamland's secrets are stored. We can only access what has been authorized for us to learn. Zorlak and his team of elders make this decision. They are his advisors in matters of this magnitude." Tara paused, and then continued, "I have selected a comfortable spot for the learning to take place and it is not very much further. We will rest for another few moments and then finish our journey." True to her word in a few moments they were on the move again and Kay began wondering why they stopped flying.

This was a long trip. As soon as that thought entered her head, she sensed the correct answer. They were all supposed to make this trek together as the group of three. They were learning and proving themselves to the secret keepers. These apparently were like guardians of the secrets stored in this vaulted room. As Tara led them through the stacks of vaults to our spot she had selected, Kay realized that the room glowed with a transparent shimmery glaze of muted shades. The comfortable area selected had huge, overstuffed chairs to sit in and an even larger screen hanging on the opposite wall.

Elizabeth and Kay both knew the mode of learning, instantly. Elizabeth finally spoke to Tara and with a tone that made Kays' blood run cold. "I hardly think this is the time for home movies. Tara, you know we don't have very much time." Elizabeth was still on her feet facing her granddaughter.

Tara's eyes were wide with surprise as she answered her grandmother "Grandma, I need for you to see some of the inhabitants and the roles they play here. This is important so we know who we can trust. I also need to show you the skeletal structure of Dreamland. This is so you can find your way back anytime we may stray from the path. This is the basic knowledge we all need in order to complete a successful journey to where we have to go. I am just making sure we know our way." Tara sat down with a thud.

Before Elizabeth could even react, the screen had lit up and there was something beginning. She too sat with a thud. The three sat in a huddle watching the brief but compact history of Dreamland as well as a detailed topographical map of the entire structure. It was cone shaped and sat on an angle on top of a blackened iron cone. This was all hollowed out to make the necessary space to grow Dreamland to what it is today. Then the next video segment was all about the potential threats out in Dreamland.

These included all the creatures that wanted to destroy Dreamland and Earth for the pure evil of it as their only reason for doing it. This was a colorful array of shapes and sizes and they all had strange names. The main idea that both Kay and Elizabeth took away from that part of the learning was that Zorlak is the big guy, Nightmare Fairies are evil and love it, Throgs are helpers to the dreamers, Yarong, keeper of the path, was always close by to assist any lost or straggling creatures. At least they had a handle on whom to avoid and who to ask for help, if necessary.

Kay realized that the one thing she didn't know yet was what the threat was. Was it a resident or a group them? Did they have anything to do with Elizabeth, Kay of Tara? Why us? She had a million questions and no time to ask. They were on their way shortly after the short information session. Tara led the way again.

They wove in and out of flowers and bushes. They avoided rivers, streams and animals. Eventually they stopped short in front of the most beautiful thing Elizabeth or Kay had ever seen. There was a bejeweled panel door that shimmered and glowed like the edges of a crystal goblet in the direct sunlight. The door shuddered and then silently slid to one side, allowing them to enter. Kay and Elizabeth both hesitated and Tara gave them an encouraging glance and they too entered the vault. Kay had thought they were already in the Inner Sanctum when they watched the video. Now she knew she had been mistaken. This was so obviously the gate to the Inner Sanctum. Kay and Elizabeth were expecting to see God himself inside this shrine.

Tara spoke as soon as the door opened all the way, "Time to enter Zenithia, the heart of Dreamland. Here is where we learn our mission. All will become clear in a few moments." Tara had just finished her sentence when a huge white shadowy figure appeared out of nowhere and was coming our way very quickly.

Chapter 17

Kay awoke in a cold sweat, tangled in her sheets and shivering all over. What had happened? She was in Zenithia and suddenly she was here. She sat up slowly trying to get the most warmth from her blanket as she rose slowly to a sitting position. She rubbed her eyes and took a deep breath. She knew where she was and why, but how did it happen so quickly? Her head was still spinning from her rapid switch in gears from deep sleep to fully awake. Something must have happened to make them send her back so fast. Sudden panic set in as Kay became frantic to determine if her daughter had been sent back with her. Kay entered her daughters' room at a dead run and spun around in a full circle. As the door gave way and she entered the room, stumbling. She found her daughter in a similar state to the way she had awoken but she was still sound asleep. Kay felt fear welling up inside her as she sat in the rocker beside her daughter's bed. As she drew in her breath slowly trying to calm herself down, her heart began to slow its pace and the feeling was back in her legs. She was listening to Tara's labored breathing, and it sounded like she was in pain. Kay was starting to get angry now. They should never have left Tara there and sent Kay back alone.

Kay began to pray for strength and vision as well as the safety of her child as well as safety for the whole world, and Dreamland. It was at that moment that Kay finally realized that not only did she believe in Dreamland but also, she knew in her core that there was a very real and powerful threat to Dreamland and she and her family were the key to its safety and its survival.

She was pondering all of this, praying and listening to Tara breath and suddenly Tara sat bolt upright and shouted "No!" at the ceiling. Kay jumped to her feet and grabbed her daughter. As she sat next to Tara, she started to rock her like a baby. Tara snuggled in and then slowly raised her head and with wide-eyed innocence she said, "Good catch, Mum" and giggled.

"Let's eat, I'm starving" Tara said grinning at her mother.

"Ok, the cooks have already been up for hours. We probably even missed breakfast." Kay smiled as she led her daughter to the kitchen.

"Any sign of the good doctor, Greta?" Kay asked the head chef.

"No ma'am, no sign for two days now," Greta replied with concern showing in her voice.

"I'm sure he is just up in his hidden library vault, or wherever it is he hides his research." Kay assured Greta it was probably nothing, but Greta persisted.

"No ma'am, bad thing, not nothing." Greta was becoming more agitated by the minute. "Dr. Cain has not been up there for years, and the bad memories are all up there. This is bad for doctor." Greta insisted.

"Ok, I'll check on him if he doesn't show up for dinner. I'm sure I could find his hideaway." Kay said soothingly.

"Ok, thank you, ma'am, Dr. Cain is a good boss and a nice man. Thank you very much ma'am." Greta gushed.

"Pancakes, and Daddy!!" Tara squealed.

Kay spun around so fast that Drew had to catch her before she hit the doorframe. "That's my favorite little calamity Jane." Drew hugged her to him and bent to kiss her.

Kay pushed her hand into his chest and said,"Hang on a minute. Why are you here, now, today? Tara did you know Daddy was coming today?" Kay was trying to regain her balance and her composure. Drew hugged her again and planted a kiss on her neck.

Tara giggled, "We really missed you, Daddy. When did Dr. Cain call you?" Tara was insistent. "Tell me, Daddy?" Tara would not give up.

Drew took a deep breath and said, "Well, pet, I don't even know myself. I just felt like I should just get in the car and drive here."

Tara giggled even harder now "I knew it would work. Daddy, you're just like us. I got you here because I thought you here," Tara finished breathlessly.

"What do you mean you thought me here, honey?" Drew asked because his curiosity was piqued.

"Well, like when I thought Momma into Dreamland to meet me and Grandma." Tara explained innocently. She had no idea that Kay hadn't told Drew about the Dreamland visits. She was afraid he would insist that they leave the Sleep Centre and come home. Drew took a long look at Kay and asked Tara if she wanted to see what he brought for her.

"What did you bring me, Daddy? Tell me, now, Daddy!" Tara was hopping up and down on each foot, two hops on each side and then the other.

"Come outside and I'll show you, pumpkin," Drew beamed at his daughter.

"Drew, darling, we need to talk. All three of us." Kay whispered to Drew as they headed for the front door and the waiting driveway.

Tara had reached the front door and, subsequently the driveway, long before Kay and Drew. They knew by the yelling and giggling they could hear that Tara had found her bicycle.

"Daddy, It's beautiful, it's perfect and I love it and you all to pieces." Tara jumped on her new bike and went around the driveway enough times to prove she could ride it and then headed for the paths behind the house with a wave and a smile.

"Now would be a great time to talk, Kay. I'm glad that Tara 'thought me here' if that is even possible. My presence here is obviously necessary, otherwise I wouldn't be here." Drew looked at Kay and he could see the strain in her face and the added years of worry in her eyes. He took one step forward and hugged his wife.

"I was going crazy without you two and I didn't think you were telling me everything on the phone. Let's go into the study and talk," Drew whispered into Kay's ear as he gently led her to the door of the study.

There was already a fire in the study, it seemed to be perpetual, but Kay had never seen anyone tending the fire. She was relieved to finally have her best friend and soul mate to share this weight with her. Now she could relax a little and try and decipher all of the information she had received in Dreamland. First, she had to tell Drew about the trips to Dreamland before Tara did, as she needed for her husband to know how well she was holding up.

He would probably be proud of her, she just hoped that he would believe her and would not try to stop she and Tara from assisting Zorlak in protecting Dreamland.

He could always help keep Dr. Cain distracted and out of their way. Tara and I could give Dr. Cain just enough information about Dreamland to convince him that Drew had dream connections to Tara and Kay also.

Kay was lost in her thoughts when Drew sat beside her, in front of the glowing fire. As he put his arm around her shoulders, he could actually feel some of the tension release from her body. He held her even closer then and she wiggled in even tighter. Kay sighed heavily and looked into the eyes of her loving husband and burst into tears. Drew held her in his arms and rocked her, just like she had just done to Tara in her bed.

Finally, the sobbing stopped, and Drew held her out at arm's length to look into her eyes again. "There's my gal, back to the land of the living. Honey, you looked like a zombie when I first got here. I think that crying helped you to vent some of your stress now, let's have it. The whole story with all the sordid details." Drew insisted.

Kay sat up and remained in her husband's arms while she slowly related the events of the past few days. Kay told him the details of the Sleep Centre, picnic and the events in Dreamland. By the time Kay had finished Drew felt like he had stepped into a science fiction movie. Alternate, lateral co-existing worlds that protect and complement each other. Now he was being asked to believe that his wife, daughter and deceased mother-in-law were going to save this world and Dreamland from certain annihilation.

Before Drew could even begin to digest these ideas, Tara had returned and wanted pancakes that only her Daddy could make for her. Tara was not about to be swayed from her desire for her father's pancakes and homemade syrup. The trio headed for the kitchen and set about making Tara's favorite breakfast for her.

"So, where is the good doctor anyway, Kay?" Drew had just completed his question when Dr. Cain appeared in the kitchen doorway.

"Good morning, all! What a beautiful spring morning." Dr. Cain reported as he entered the kitchen to find Drew helping Greta with breakfast. He only hesitated a moment before crossing the floor to shake Drew's hand and welcome him to the Sleep Centre.

"Good morning, Dr. Cain. It is so good to see you. Are my girls driving you crazy yet?" Drew asked jokingly.

"Not at all Drew. I have been enjoying their company. I do regret, however our lack of progress with the assessment of Tara and her dreams so far. It seems that there are always too many distractions." Dr. Cain stated in a frustrated tone.

Drew and Kay exchanged knowing glances but remained silent as Tara chattered on. Breakfast was finally ready, and they sat together in the bright, sunny nook and ate together in silence.

Chapter 18

Finally, their breakfast eaten, they all retired to the study to talk and drink their coffee. This had been the place of much feverish activity over the past few days, but no one knew what the other had experienced within these walls. Dr. Cain had encountered his own set of interesting phenomena, unbeknownst to Kay or Tara. While they, too had some fascinating episodes, unknown to Dr. Cain. Now, Drew had arrived. Dr. Cain wasn't sure if he should be concerned or not. He was, however being extremely cautious of his behavior. One of the many things Kay had shared with Drew was the fact that neither she nor her mother were exactly sure yet if Dr. Cain was one of the good guys or bad guys. Everyone was being more careful, even the good doctor.

Drew watched the interaction between Dr. Cain and the women in his life through curious eyes. He didn't miss a move, glance or sigh but he still didn't feel like he had learned a single thing. He knew he had seen and heard it all but felt no wiser. If anything, he felt like he suddenly knew less, rather than more. It seemed like the longer you stayed here the less you felt you knew. The Sleep Centre had a way of making people sleepy. Drew could no longer hold his lids open. He needed some sleep, and soon.

Kay stood and said to Tara and Dr. Cain, "I'm taking Daddy in to show him where he can get some sleep. It looks like he had a long day." Then she and Drew were both gone.

"So, little lady, what have you and your lovely Mother been up to these past few days?" Dr. Cain asked Tara, point blank.

"Nothing," was all Tara could muster.

"That sounds like a little white lie, my dear." Dr. Cain scolded.

Tara was immediately uncomfortable with this entire situation. She really didn't like the look in Dr. Cain's eyes or the tone of his voice. Her 'squiggly senses were 'glowing' inside her chest, her head and her stomach. These weird feelings inside her were starting to make her feel like a superhero or something. Tara knew instinctively that this was evil, and the Nightmare Fairies couldn't be far away. She shuddered and then was suddenly filled with a warmth she could not describe.

"Dr. Cain we had a girl's day and we just relaxed and enjoyed our time together." Tara stated defiantly.

"Well now, aren't we grown up?" Dr. Cain retorted with a grin. He knew when he had been outsmarted and this was a perfect example. He had to watch his step a little more carefully in front of Tara, he thought to himself; she was sharper than her years would make you think.

"We talked about girl stuff mostly, anyway." Tara recovered cutely.

Kay appeared in the doorway to find the good doctor staring at Tara in a very quizzical way. He seemed to be almost lost in her gaze and she wasn't even looking at him. Tara was staring out the window watching the brightly colored birds playing in the birdbath.

"So, that was a real surprise, wasn't it Dr. Cain, Tara?" Kay offered.

"Yes, indeed it was, my dear," Dr. Cain retorted with a grunt.

"Is there something wrong Dr. Cain?" Kay was confused by his sudden hostility toward her husband.

"I sense some hostility here, Dr. Cain. Is there something wrong with Drew being here?" Kay asked trying to hide her impatience.

"I thought we agreed not to have Drew visit until I had made my initial assessment of Tara?" Dr. Cain snapped.

"I didn't call him here, Tara thought him here." Kay said defensively.

Tara jumped right in then, "It's true Dr. Cain. I just kept thinking about Daddy coming here to visit then he finally came here." Tara stated in a matter-of-fact tone.

Dr. Cain was stunned. He had read about this type of strong familial connection between two or more conscious minds of extremely close relatives. But he had never before witnessed it, until now. If what they were saying was true, Dr. Cain being a trained scientist, who had just observed the perfect telepathic incident. This was a major breakthrough for the psychic scientists in their collective quest for validation and acceptance. This could make the difference in research funding grants for several years to come. This phenomenon had to be researched, and by him, regardless of the fact it was a stretch from his brain wave and dream wave research. Maybe, it wasn't really all that different. He would need a couple of research assistants and a secretary in addition to the two nurses and one paramedic he already employed at the Sleep Centre. Not to mention three chefs, a maid or two, a gardener and a handyman. He only then realized he already had a fair-sized staff. He would make some calls and check out the talent that might be available in the research world. There were still other, prominent Scientists that would kill to be part of this new research project.

With the real-life examples Dr. Cain already had at his disposal, it was the perfect choice to have him lead the team.

Kay could tell that Dr. Cain was about to do his disappearing act again. At least they had Drew to bounce ideas off now; they needed time alone with Drew. As Kay began to speak, in waltzed Drew. "Well, Dr. Cain, it really sounds like you need some time to organize something, so why don't I take these two lovely ladies for a picnic in the woods. We'll be gone for hours, so take your time." Drew said over his shoulder as he draped his arms around Kay and Tara and headed for the kitchen. "We will need to get a picnic basket ready. Come on now ladies pitch in, I could use a hand." Drew shot over his shoulder again as he headed for the wall sized fridge. "I am making a very special picnic for us today. We need some family time and I'm going to make sure we have that. I want you two to take me to where you had your picnic, with the flowers and the butterflies," Drew finished with a bow.

The three chefs, who slept off the kitchen, heard the noise and all came running to assist. Drew stood his ground, made them sit with Kay and Tara. He had decided it was show time. He truly needed to lighten the mood that he felt settling over the entire property. Now he was starting to act all funny like the women in his life. Was it the family he had married into? He had been warned that the Beauregarde's had quite an eccentric history, here in Atlanta. There were two versions of the family history, one from the family and the other from the psychiatrists that had tried to help their family.

They had huge hearts but there was weird stuff that had gone on at that mansion on the hill. Drew had read all the stories trying to prepare for his own father's condescending attitude toward the entire Beauregarde ancestry.

His family was not exactly their best friends, ever. He didn't have time to think about that now, he had to get his family out of range of this house and into the woods where they could talk, in private.

Drew had a premium picnic made for three in no time flat. Even the head chef smiled at his speed, accuracy, and creativity. "Ok, ladies, it's time to hit the trail." Drew bellowed as he herded the two of them out into the morning sun and waiting path to picnic heaven.

Kay and Tara raced to the open doorway to the front yard and the path to the woods. They almost collided when they arrived within a fraction of a second of each other. Tara ran for her new bike, giggling all the way. Kay sat, winded on the bottom step, waiting for Drew. Tara met her parents at the path to the woods; she was waiting for them when they arrived, hand in hand.

"This is just like before I got sick. We used to go out every weekend for walks in the park and the woods. It's been a really long time since we did this, huh, Momma?" Tara sighed. "Good we can do it today, then isn't it?" Tara continued, "I'll go ahead on the path and watch for creatures." Tara stated and then disappeared down the path.

Drew looked into Kay's eyes and knew that he was not quite ready yet for the whole truth, but he was going to get it. He tried to prepare himself as best he could, but he knew the whole time it was useless.

He had learned over the years with this family that he could never imagine the stuff they would tell him or how he would react to it. "Let's just enjoy the walk, honey?" Kay said lovingly as she put her arm around his waist. Drew gently threw his arm over his wife's shoulder they headed for the woods.

"We'll talk after we eat, ok? I want to relax a bit first too." Drew said as he hugged her shoulder even closer, and they continued silently to the picnic spot Kay and Tara had discovered.

When they all arrived at the picnic site, they spread the blanket, and all took a seat in a circle with the basket in the middle and settled in for their feast.

Meanwhile, back at the Sleep Centre, Dr. Cain was up to his usual madness. He was holed up in his attic fortress, researching until he nearly went blind. He would only ever be permitted to go so far into Dreamland and would never know all of its abilities. The Nightmare Fairies were also up to their same old distasteful tricks, on the good Doctor.

All in all, it was shaping up to be a regular yet unusual day, again. Everything appeared to be in their proper place and all happy in their dreams. Life looked normal and peaceful.

That in and of itself was a very frightening thought for all sides involved. Unfortunately, it wasn't going to stay that way, not for too long, anyway.

Chapter 19

During their picnic Drew had some time to try and digest the information Kay and Tara had started to relay to him. He was still having great difficulty with the fact that his lovely wife seemed to now believe in Dreamland. He found this unsettling and reassuring at the same time. His feelings were confusing him almost as much as all the strange dreams they had told him about. His wife and daughter were talking about their dreams like they were visits somewhere. The fact that Tara and Elizabeth had always spoken of Dreamland like it was a real place had never really concerned him before, because he had always thought, as did Kay, that it was only a children's story Elizabeth told to entertain Tara.

When Drew finally spoke, Kay was almost at her wit's end. She had no idea what thoughts and questions had been going through his head and she was concerned that he may think they were both crazy. She really couldn't blame him if he did, at least until she and Tara explained their experiences in more detail.

"I must say, Kay, that I am really proud of your new adventurous nature and your open mindedness regarding Dreamland. I never thought I would live to see the day that the mere mention of Dreamland didn't send you into uncontrollable fits of shaking. Tara's excitement does not really surprise me, though it is nice to see you two so committed to this joint dream, or whatever it is. I am confused though. How can Dreamland possibly be a real place and how in hell could your dead mother be there?" Drew took in a deep breath, as he looked deep into Kay's eyes for the truth.

"Well..." Kay began tentatively, "I'm not really sure Drew how any of it is possible. All I know is that I need to help Tara interpret her dreams in order to save Dreamland and the world. I know," Kay raised an open hand and placed her fingers on Drew's lips to silence him as she continued "I thought we were all nuts at first, but when I saw my mother, I knew that all the things she had told me over the years about Dreamland were true. She had been trying to involve me for years, but I always resisted." Kay stopped for a breath.

"Basically, Tara and I are going to have very vivid dreams that will teach each of us what our role is to be in this dire situation Dreamland is in. There is a weakness in the fiber that separates the two worlds and Tara, Mother and I must find it and repair it before anything can damage it further." Kay finished in a hopeful tone.

Drew just sat there in the woods looking at his beautiful wife and daughter and trying to figure out how in the hell they got into this situation in the first place. Finally, he spoke cautiously, "Kay, I know your mother has talked about Dreamland for years, but now you are telling me it is a real place and not a story. I am trying to digest all of this, but I still can't see why Tara 'thought' me here. Is there a role for me to play in Dreamland or am I here to protect you both while you are dreaming?" Drew was becoming exasperated now.

"Well." Kay began again, "We were hoping you could help us to distract Dr. Cain and keep him on the wrong track while we do this, so he doesn't find out too much and mess things up. If he figures out the dream content and meanings before we do, then he could do more harm than good. Also, mother said that the Nightmare Fairies are helping to keep him on the wrong track. They will definitely make sure that he won't get far enough into Dreamland to even begin to unravel any of the secrets of Dreamland." Kay finished with a heavy sigh. "I am just so glad you are here for me to lean on and to talk to, Drew." Kay reached over and squeezed both of his hands at once.

Drew moved closer so that he could wrap his arms around Kay as he said "I will do whatever you and Tara and Elizabeth need me to do to help with this unbelievable situation. I hope when this is all over, we can go back to a semi normal life at least. For now, let's enjoy our picnic." Drew finished reassuringly.

The rest of their day passed quickly as they followed Tara on her bike around the numerous woodland trails. They saw flowers, birds, streams and amazing wildlife as they meandered back toward the Sleep Centre. Drew thought that the centre looked like a turn of the century manor that he had seen in old pictures his own mother had shown him in his youth. He couldn't possibly be right about that though because his parents had only moved to Atlanta when he was born. He made a mental note to himself to look for the old pictures in the attic when they returned home. In the meantime, he would have his hands full with Dreamland and all of its messages from beyond. He was starting to feel like the unlikely victim in a horror movie and it was starting to make him a little nervous.

As the threesome entered the main door of the Sleep Centre, they could hear Greta screaming from the kitchen. It sounded like a tribe of banshee's was attacking her. Drew bolted straight to the kitchen to find her holding Dr. Cain's head in her hands, kneeling on the floor, covered in blood.

He slid to a stop and knelt beside Dr. Cain and Greta, "What the hell happened here?" Drew asked breathlessly.

Greta, sobbing, tried to explain "Dr. Cain... he fell... he was talking to himself... not looking... hit his head on the counter..."

Kay ran to the clinic on the east side of the centre to get a nurse to help Dr. Cain and Tara sat on the floor beside her father holding Dr. Cain's hand and rocking. When Kay returned with the nurse, she could hear her daughter saying over and over to Dr. Cain "They didn't mean to hurt you. They don't understand, that's all"

The nurse, Cynthia, managed to raise Dr. Cain's head just enough to know he was going to need stitches, but first they had to stop the bleeding. Drew got her an ice pack and some towels. After several long, tense moments the bleeding started to slow down and Dr. Cain's eyes fluttered open, but only for a second, and he squeezed Tara's hand.

Tara patted the back of Dr. Cain's hand as she crooned in her best adult voice, "It will be all right now. They didn't mean to hurt you. They were just playing. Rest now and we'll get you all fixed up good as new." Tara finished with a shy smile.

Kay and Drew were dumbfounded by their daughters' behavior as she helped the nurse get the doctor onto a stretcher and wheel him into the infirmary portion of the Sleep Centre. Tara just looked at her parents and smiled.

Kay, Drew and Tara retired to the study and just sat staring at the fire for a long time trying to process what they had all just witnessed. Kay was relieved at least that Dr. Cain could not interrogate Drew any further tonight on his mysterious arrival at the centre.

Greta came into the study to let them know that Dr. Cain was resting comfortably, and that Cynthia had put in eight stitches in his head to close his wound. Greta assured them that the good doctor would be fine after a good night's sleep.

She nodded at Drew and Kay and left the room, no doubt to go hover over Dr. Cain all night. Off Greta went to do just that and so Dr. Cain slept in the Infirmary all night with Cynthia and Greta watching over him. Since it had been such a long day for everyone Kay and Drew tucked Tara in together and went to Kay's room. The feather bed was the perfect size for the two of them. As they snuggled in under the comforter, they both heaved a huge sigh of relief.

"Drew, darling, you have no idea how much I have missed you in the past few days." Kay exclaimed she could wait no longer. She threw her arms around his neck and kissed him fully on the mouth. Drew was stunned by her adventurous behavior, maybe the Sleep Centre might not be so bad for her after all. Drew just held her close, kissed her and hung on as tightly as he could and smiled to himself.

Finally, Drew spoke "Kay there is a great deal more that I know you need to tell me, but for tonight can we just cuddle up and go to sleep. I love you and I really just want to snuggle. Okay?" he whispered.

Kay was more than happy to oblige. She kissed her husband on the cheek, cuddled into the crook of his arm and drifted off to sleep. Unfortunately for Kay she was immediately whisked off to Zenithia in Dreamland to complete the machinations of the previous night. The good part was that Tara, and her mother were already they're waiting for her.

Chapter 20

When Dr. Cain woke up the next morning he had little to no memory of the events of the night before. He could feel the tightness of the stitches in his head but had no idea how they had gotten there. He did feel rested for the first time in days, maybe he could actually make some progress today, after all, now he had a new subject to assist in his research. Dr. Cain was actually glad that Drew had arrived at the Sleep Centre. He had a feeling that he would need to monitor the interaction of the whole family in order to get to the bottom of this strange phenomenon. He was so excited at the prospect of this new psychic incident of Tara and Drew's that he could hardly contain himself. As soon as they were out the front door to go on their daily picnic, Dr. Cain bolted for the attic library. It seemed that the more time he spent with this family the more strange things occurred. He set aside his Sleep Centre property research for the time being so he could focus on this newest development. He began by documenting his observations of the daughter and father and how it was just accepted that she had 'thought' him there. They acted like it happened all the time. Dr. Cain began a list of detailed questions he needed to ask Drew, Kay and Tara regarding this ability of Tara's. He needed to know how many times it had happened before, if ever and was it only with her father or could she do this with other family members? He had so many questions he couldn't write them down as fast as he was thinking them up.

When Dr. Cain had completed his preliminary list of questions he went to his online directory of Scientists and their current projects. He located a Dr. Borja who was doing telepathic research in Amsterdam.

It appeared that he had been investigating the very type of occurrence that Dr. Cain had witnessed today. Dr. Cain sent him an email asking Dr. Borja if he had any documented cases that he had witnessed himself and waited for his reply. Within minutes Dr. Borja emailed Dr. Cain back to express his interest in the incident that he had explained to him in the email about Tara and her father. Dr. Borja had read about cases where, with very close family members, they could convey thoughts to one another but never make then actually come to where they were. For the next several hours Dr. Borja and Dr. Cain compared notes on their research projects ranging from telekinesis to dream research and back to Tara and her father. The two doctors had decided to share their research in an attempt to speed up the remote viewing of Tara's dreams. Dr. Cain was concerned that if he didn't complete his new computer program to add dimension to a person's thought waves in dreams, he may lose his chance. Tara was, by far, the very best subject either of these doctors had ever come across.

What Dr. Cain didn't know was that Zorlak, thanks to the Nightmare Fairies, knew that the good doctor was seeking assistance to speed up his dream research. Tara was also acutely aware of Dr. Cain's newfound curiosity regarding her ability to 'think' her father into doing things. Tara had never really thought that this ability was different. She thought everyone could get what they wanted if they really wanted it badly enough.

By the end of the day the two doctors had agreed that Dr. Borja should come to Atlanta. He would be bringing his research assistant to help set up all of the research before the rest of their team arrived. They would be bringing all of his files, case studies and video statements so that they could pool their resources.

They were both cognizant of the fact that time was running out and they needed answers before Tara and her parents left the Sleep Centre. Dr. Borja had the resources of the European Psychic

Research Foundation behind him and Dr. Cain could use all of the resources he could get his hands on and as quickly as possible.

Dr. Cain sat back and congratulated himself on his plan to include a psychic expert into his dream research. Especially in light of Tara's newly exposed psychic ability, or whatever it was. Ruthie would have been proud of him because she had always wanted him to include other doctors and scientists in his research projects. She felt he could have benefited from not only another point of view but also from funding dollars that were available for joint endeavors.

Dr. Cain began organizing his Sleep Centre site research while he pondered his new partnership with Dr. Borja. He was really hoping that this new doctor would be able to shed some light on the abilities Tara had displayed as well as maybe even her dream content. Dr. Cain had been focusing on the interpretation and viewing of Tara's dreams and Dr. Borja's expertise lay in the field of psychic phenomenon.

Dr. Borja was also very excited at the prospect of working with the, now infamous, Dr. Cain. He had studied Dr. Cain's early research work with infants and young children. This had been a large area of study for Dr. Borja for the past several years. He too would benefit greatly from this new partnership, that is as long as it was successful. Dr. Borja was aware of the reputation Dr. Cain had in the research world for being difficult to work with. Dr. Borja, having a very similar reputation, was not the least bit concerned as to whether or not they would get along.

There was no question in his mind that having the same goal and personality type. They would work together with a speed and efficiency they would be proud of at any age. Neither of them were young men anymore and both blacklisted in their own scientific circles, this was the second chance they had both been preparing for ever since their early years of study.

This was the chance of a lifetime and Dr. Cain was keenly aware of this fact. Dr. Borja would be here in just three short days. Dr. Cain needed to get all of the Sleep Centre location research together immediately so he could pass it off to one of the new research assistants Dr. Borja was bringing with him. That meant he would be up all night and the next day just on that project. He had years of historical and geographical anomalies in the area surrounding the Sleep Centre. This was aside from all of the histories of all the families that had ever inhabited the ancient mansion, he had recently uncovered in his attic hide away. The Sleep Centre site itself was famous during several years of civil war that had plagued the region in the 17 and 1800's.

Dr. Cain set up a small space in the corner of his attic office, closest to doorway, yet still inside, where it would be safe from harm. He took great pains to pack up all of his maps, diagrams and books full of family histories, all in catalogued order in a huge floor to ceiling shelving unit that Dr. Cain had reserved for some of his more recent work. This was no time to moon over directions not yet taken, he was thinking too much about Ruthie now.

He wasn't sure if that was to comfort him or to put him on his guard so no one could hurt him with his own research ever again. Either way it had served both purposes lately, so he made a conscious decision to take comfort from his wife's presence and also stay on guard for potential threats.

Dr. Cain was forced then to re-evaluate his entire research focus and how it could change. He would have no choice but to share the credit for his own hard work and near genius ideas. The sudden fear of losing control and credit for one's own ideas numbed him for a moment as his thoughts returned to how he had almost gone to jail for his research just twenty years ago.

No other Scientist or scientific organization was even remotely interested in a joint endeavor with Dr. Cain, the 'brainiacal' doctor, not for years now. Most of his old colleagues didn't even know that he had heard them referring to him as that for several years before he had been officially blacklisted and everyone knew. Dr. Cain just sort of faded from view, but he never stopped searching for the connection he knew existed between the adult parents' brains and the brainpower of the offspring brain. He had been so close and then they yanked his funding out from under him. He lost a state-of-the-art sleep facility and thirty full time research assistants, not to mention his reputation and career. Hopefully, his new partnership would give his research the momentum it had needed to fuel his breakthrough to fruition and prove to everyone that he was a superior scientist.

Dr. Cain became so immersed in his re-organization of this research that he lost track of time. His stomach started to rumble at one point, so he made himself a cup of tea and ate a biscuit he had brought up there with him.

He only realized the time when he heard the peel of the Sunday service Church bells. How could it possibly be Sunday already? He only had a day and a half to get ready for his colleagues' arrival. He had not even seen his patient and her family let alone advised them of Dr. Borja's impending arrival and all of the new tests and strategies they could employ together. Dr. Cain realized that the next twelve hours had to be dedicated to the Prescott family before he lost the main focus of his research. He only had a small amount of time to get the family on board with the new tests. That is when it finally occurred to him that the patient or her family might not even allow additional testing when he hadn't even been able to complete a full evaluation of Tara yet.

The child had been in his centre for over a week now and still no actual hands-on research or testing had been done. Dr. Cain had to really rack up the test times with Tara now before Dr. Borja arrived and decided that the project could not really be that important to him if he hadn't even done measurable base testing on her. How could he obtain the results he needed in time to properly impress his new partner? He couldn't even think straight as he stumbled down the long hallway to the secret stairway from his attic to his room on the main floor. This had helped more than just Dr. Cain in slipping in and out of the other rooms in the manor undetected. When Dr. Cain was safely in his room and showered, he dressed as professionally as he could with nervous hands. He got ready to join Drew in the study, where he had spent a great deal of time since his arrival. Something about the signal for his laptop only worked in that room and he was reluctant to share his work he did on it. Dr. Cain had bigger things on his mind as he got two of his favorite cigars and headed for the study to interrogate his first member of the Prescott family.

He had to convince Drew of the benefits of his new research and how his new partnership could help Tara.

Dr. Cain had been right about Drew. There he was in front of the roaring fire with his coffee in one hand and his other hand running through his thick dark hair.

"Good afternoon, Drew, and how are you on this beautiful day?" Dr. Cain bellowed.

Drew jumped at least six inches out of his overstuffed chair as he exclaimed, "Dr. Cain, are you trying to give me a heart attack or something. You scared the hell out of me. Until then I was in the middle of a writer's block. By the way, where have you been for the past day and a half? You do know it is Sunday now, don't you?" Drew finished with a wave to Dr. Cain to sit down.

"I have stumbled across some extremely interesting scientific phenomenon regarding the events that brought you to the Sleep

Centre." Dr. Cain took this opportunity to plunge right in and spit out as much as he could before Drew started asking too many questions. "I really want to explain it to you while the girls are out for their walk." He finished hopefully.

"Well Dr. Cain, I would love to be of assistance, but the girls are actually napping not out for their walk. They actually haven't been for a walk in days, but you would have known that if you were ever around. I think it is high time for you to come clean and let me in on the big mystery you think you have uncovered." Drew took a deep exhausted breath and continued, "I want to know exactly what your plans and intentions are with my daughter. How much longer you are going to expect us to stay in this crazy mansion? I have not seen you even have a conversation with Tara since I arrived and that was three days ago." Drew finished in an exasperated tone and started to stand up from his seat.

"Well, I have had a great deal of information that relates directly to your family's past and this particular property." Dr. Cain began tentatively. "I have been finding so much related information I have allowed myself to get a little bogged down in it. I am truly sorry for the inconvenience I have caused your family; I just keep getting bombarded by the ability of your daughter. I have never seen anyone think someone into coming where they were. Please tell me how many times you have done this in the past with Tara? Or has she been able to get you to bring specific items to her or call at a certain time?" Dr. Cain stopped only to catch his breath again to continue.

Drew raised his hand up palm, facing Dr. Cain and said, "Stop! I will not have our life dissected, nor will I tolerate you prying into our past family history. We are here for one thing and one thing only. Help my daughter sleep soundly without the terror and confusion of her dreams and do it fast. I am giving you one week to wrap up whatever research you are doing and help my child or we will be gone regardless." Drew stormed out of the study and into his own room that he shared with his wife.

Kay was in a restless sleep, so Drew knew she was in this crazy Dreamland or somewhere and all he needed was to lie beside her and hold her in his arms to help her settle down and also to ease his own mind. Drew was still kicking himself for ever letting them come here without him. He had taken a sabbatical from work for a month, but he was not subjecting his family to another month of this ridiculous torture. When Kay woke up Drew would be able to talk to her about his reasons for being distraught over this entire situation.

He hoped that she would agree with leaving here in one week if nothing had happened to further a cure for their daughter. He snuggled into his wife's back and pulled cotton knitted blanket over both of them. Kay settled down almost immediately and not long after that Drew was fast asleep. Drew didn't even think about what might be going on in Dreamland, after all Kay was taking care of things there, at least he hoped she was.

Tara slept soundly in her little room entirely oblivious to the chaos and turmoil in her father's thoughts. She was just content to be in Dreamland with her mother and grandmother, finally.

Chapter 21

As soon as Kay arrived in Zenithia she was immediately aware of the reason they had been sent back so abruptly the previous night. Lutharious had somehow managed to find out that someone was there with Zorlak and that it could be the 'little one'. Zorlak wasn't taking any chances, so he had sent Kay back and had hidden Tara in his cloak until Lutharious had been removed from Zenithia. Lutharious was becoming bolder as evidenced by his barging into Zenithia. Only those who were invited or taken there were welcome to enter. Zorlak had Lutharious taken to the dungeons so that he could be detained for long enough that Zorlak could discuss things with Kay, Elizabeth and Tara as soon as possible.

Kay was worried about this new development, but she had renewed strength since Drew had arrived at the Sleep Centre to stay with them and she knew she was now ready to take on the challenges that Zorlak had for her. Lutharious was becoming bolder daily and the Throgs had still not managed to locate the weakness that he had spoken of.

Zorlak had ordered a renewed effort in determining where Lutharious was getting his information regarding the presence of the "little one" Zorlak needed to be able to guarantee the safety of Tara and her relatives or there would be no hope left at all, for any of them. Lutharious must be stopped and Tara's presence there was imperative, but only if he could protect her. She needed to remain safe at all costs.

The Throgs had been very busy following Lutharious and his spies in an effort to determine how he was getting his information. They had come to the conclusion that they had a spy of their own they should be searching for. The Throgs were starting to not trust anyone, so Zorlak demanded a meeting with them.

Tara and her family should be here any moment so they could be included in the discussion with the Throgs. Maybe Tara could sense something that the Throgs were missing. Tara knew Dreamland inside out now after visiting so much in the past three days.

It was truly amazing to both Kay and Elizabeth that Tara was of exceptional mental and psychic abilities. Kay found herself wondering how many of these abilities her daughter was able to avail of in the real world. She was constantly surprising herself with how easily she was settling into her new role as Dreamland saviors' mother. She had issues with the fear of the mere thought of Dreamland but whenever she visited there it seemed so natural, she forgot to be afraid. This was what her own mother, Elizabeth had been talking about when she had told Kay she would get so used to being in Dreamland that one day she would forget she even lived topside, in the 'real' world. Kay marveled at the fact that she was flying down a hallway towards a meeting with Zorlak, the Dream keeper and that her daughter was necessary for the existence of both Earth and Dreamland.

Zorlak had managed to gather up all of the Throgs that were not out following a potential information source, and they were whispering amongst themselves when the main attraction flew in. The Throgs were good stalkers because they could blend in with almost anything, which meant that they could almost disappear into the sides of the walls as they searched, but whenever they saw Tara, they all got a little flustered. No girl had really been around the Throgs before, and they just weren't used to seeing any yet.

Now, in flew three of them and the collective gasp could be heard all around the alter area in Zenithia. Zorlak stood up tall at the alter and commanded all to gather near and listen carefully. The Throgs came closer and awaited the landing of their savior and her family. They were sure she could save Dreamland and they wanted to be involved in it somehow. Zorlak stretched up even taller as he bellowed for the Throgs to be quiet and to listen.

Zorlak's voice boomed, "It is imperative that we protect this child and her family members throughout this entire ordeal. We must gather around her and see her safely to the end of her mission and our ultimate fate will unveil itself to us. We are the network that will assist in saving our land and that of Tara and her family on Earth. The Squiggles will assist Tara while she makes her quest to the inner room where the sacred sphere is waiting to release the bead of power to its necessary ally. Tara is the only one with the capacity to absorb and unleash the power within the bead and save us all. Our job is to get her there and back safely. Then and only then will the three of them be equipped to heal the tear in the fabric of time that separates us from the other modes of existence that surround us and are threatening to destroy us." Zorlak took a deep breath and continued to Kay, Tara and Elizabeth only "Some outside source must have given Lutharious the knowledge he needed to feel the existence of Tara and to locate the tear so he can destroy us all. There is one more part of our plan that had become imperative to our existence. Kay, your husband Drew also has a minor connection to us here in Dreamland. He is keeping Dr. Cain at bay right now, but his role must be broadened if we are to stave off Dr. Cain's discovery until our mission is complete." Zorlak took a breath and then waved for the crowd to disperse.

"Ladies, there is much work to be done and we only have one and a half more earth days before your doctors colleague arrives."

"Then the Sleep Centre will become a pure hazard for Tara and the Nightmare Fairies. The new Doctor that is coming to the Sleep

Centre is a real threat to all of us here and on your world too. He specializes in psychic abilities and the strange phenomenon stemming from this field of study. He has been informed of Tara and the fact that she is the very best test subject either of these doctors has ever gotten their hands on. Now that they will be working together their work could seriously impair our ability to move between these worlds undetected. That would be disastrous for our current venture as we need for you to be on your world and conscious every day and here at night. Having an afternoon nap has really sped up Tara's learning curve and Kay's naps are giving her strength that she will need very soon." Zorlak stopped and stared into Tara's eyes "Are you afraid my little one?" He asked her quietly.

"No sir, I am only excited for my newest adventure to begin. I really want to save Dreamland and Earth. How soon will we be able to start my journey to the inner light bead?" Tara stopped and just stared at him with her wide eyes.

"I think it will be a great deal sooner than we first anticipated. We are closing in on the weakened fabric area. We should have its exact location before you return for your evening visit." Zorlak finished comfortably. He was impressed by her eagerness, and he knew she had been fully apprised of the situation and all of the inherent risks that could be involved. He still had misgivings about involving such a little one. The early prophets had mentioned one of beauty, youth and amazing insight that would arrive in time to save our worlds, but Tara was even more than he had hoped for. This time it had to work it just had to.

Elizabeth was restlessly standing in the shadows and just listening to Zorlak. She too had misgivings, only hers centred on Drew and his inability to imagine anything out of the ordinary.

Elizabeth had always sensed some psychic ability in Drew, but she also knew he had a major reluctance to become involved in anything remotely related to Dreamland. "Kay, darling" Elizabeth began hesitantly "Do you think Drew is really ready to become involved in this entire process with us?" Elizabeth held her breath waiting for the answer from her daughter.

Kay was pondering this and answered slowly "Mother, I think that at this point Drew would pack up and move into Dreamland if he thought it would help Tara get better. I think he may really be helpful." Kay finished sounding a great deal more confident than she felt at this moment.

"If you think so sweetie. I hope you can convince him to get involved." Elizabeth responded quietly and hugged her daughter.

"Well, I will find out this afternoon, when Tara and I get back and we can discuss it further on our evening visit. I know he wants to help solve whatever issues Tara has that are giving her these nightmares." Kay finished in a silent huff.

"Well, I think we have stayed in one spot long enough ladies, shall we move closer to the inner room now?" Zorlak suggested quietly.

As Zorlak led the way down the hidden staircase, deeper into Dreamland's core Tara became animated and very excited. Kay became more silent as she listened and strained to hear any unusual sounds and Elizabeth was breathing deeply in an effort to force herself to think more calmly.

Her daughter and granddaughter would need her help very soon and she needed her wits about her.

None of them dared to speak. It was obvious that they were going somewhere sacred, and they needed to remain undetected to succeed. They all knew that none of them could imagine what may lie ahead but they all were prepared to face it head on.

Chapter 22

Kay woke up all snuggled into her husband Drew. She could hardly believe her eyes because he never took an afternoon nap with her. She gently nudged him, and he smiled as he held her closer to his chest. "Well, I guess I'm no longer the only adult sleepy head in the family now am I, Drew?" Kay teased.

Drew wrestled her over onto her back and kissed her deeply. "I love you so much sweetheart." He murmured into her hair. "Let's get up now and find our little darling and get some grub, I'm starved." Drew said as he yanked the comforter off of his wife and gently dragged her out of the small bed.

"Uppy, uppy time sleepy heads." Tara squealed as she bounded into the room and up onto the bed. "I'm hungry, let's eat." She giggled up at her parents and then jumped off the bed and ran towards the kitchen.

By the time Kay and Drew caught up to her in the kitchen she had a mouthful of crackers and was reaching for the bottle of jam on the shelf. Greta was pleased to see her little Angel. That is what Greta started calling her all of a sudden.

Kay was just so happy to have her husband with them now. She felt so much stronger with him, near her.

Drew was very curious this afternoon. All through their late lunch he had been making strange comments about the Sleep Centre.

Kay was beginning to think that he was getting more involved on his own and she would not even have to convince him. At least she could now tell her mother that she had been right, and Drew was anxious to help in whatever way he could.

"You know, honey, I have been retyping your notes from your Dreamland visits." Drew said offhandedly.

"What?" was all Kay could get out.

"Cool Daddy!" Tara yelped "Is that on your lap computer?"

"Yes, Tara, it is on my laptop computer." Drew responded with a giggle.

"Well then, Mr. Writer, what do you think so far?" Kay asked, teasing him now.

"I think it is all a bunch of crazy dreams. That does not mean I won't help. I would do anything to speed up this assessment and treatment so we can all go home." Drew finished and smiled at Tara and Kay.

"Great, then Tara and I can join you in the study and we can see what you have figured out so far." Kay said cheerfully.

Drew and Kay stood and grabbed their coffee mugs. While they were freshening their coffee, Tara was explaining, that they would be in the study, to Greta so she wouldn't worry.

They settled in for an afternoon of brainstorming and note review. Drew took his spot in one of the overstuffed chairs in front of the roaring fire and Kay took the other. Tara sat in between them on the rug and started to talk.

She was so excited about her new role as savior of Dreamland. She was overwhelmed with all of the new knowledge she had gained in Dreamland, and it had only taken a few well-orchestrated visits. If it hadn't been for Zorlak and his training schedule she would not be so well informed. As she rambled on about all of the strange things she was experiencing there, Drew typed feverishly on his laptop. She explained about the Squigglies who were trying to interfere with Lutharious's ability to detect strangers in Dreamland. She went on to explain how the Throgs protected her by circling around her wherever she went and hiding her as best they could. She described all of the new friends she had made, and Drew was mesmerized by the detail she was able to recall.

If this was just a bunch of dreams, then how could she have imagined all of these details? Everything seemed so very clear to Tara, and she was able to explain events and concepts that were well beyond her years. She shouldn't even know about the evil in the world at only seven years of age. Drew was thinking all of these things while he busily typed her every word. Drew decided that he should review all of these notes alone after she and Kay had gone to bed, or Dreamland, or wherever they went in their sleep. The one phenomenon that stumped him was how his wife and daughter could share the same dreams. He decided that he had no choice other than to believe in the dreams and Dreamland if he was going to help speed things up here. He could only imagine how excited Dr. Cain must be at the mere prospect of all of Tara's abilities. Drew had never really thought his family was any stranger than any other. He now had cause to rethink this theory of his.

By the time Tara had told her father all of the things she thought he needed to know to help them she was mentally exhausted. Kay took her upstairs and gave her a bath to relax her and then gently tucked her into bed.

Kay would join her in Dreamland soon enough, but first she had to talk to Drew about all of this new information he had just received.

When Kay returned an hour later to the study, she found Drew reading all of the notes he had typed that afternoon and evening. They had even gotten Greta to bring them in soup and sandwiches as they worked through dinnertime. Kay didn't really like the look on Drew's face. He looked worried now and that was what Kay had been dreading. Now, he may be reluctant to help them complete their task in Dreamland. This would be disastrous, so Kay settled back into her chair next to Drew and softly asked "So, what do you really think of all this. Honey?"

"Well, for starters I have no choice but to believe all of it. I can't really fathom some of the concepts, but I guess they must be easier for Tara as she is so young. You, Kay, are you convinced that all of this stuff is real?" Drew finished weakly.

"Well, Drew, I am in the same boat as you. I have to but I'm not really sure of all of it yet." Kay hoped she sounded more confident than she felt.

"Exactly how dangerous is all of this saving Dreamland and the Earth, as our lovely daughter puts it?" Drew asked tentatively.

"I'm not really sure what you mean. According to Zorlak, if we don't succeed, then it's all over for the Earth and Dreamland, forever. I guess that makes it pretty serious, but as far as dangerous, I don't think we are in any more danger than anyone else is." Kay finished.

Kay was thinking to herself that she had been a great deal more honest and forthright than she really intended to be. She hoped it didn't scare Drew, too much.

"Besides, Mother is there to take care of us and so are Zorlak and the others." Kay continued, hopefully

"Well, Kay I do not like this very much. I can't be there to make sure you two, or should I say three, are all right. I guess I will have to keep an eye on things around here." Drew finished sounding somewhat disheartened.

"I'm really glad you said that, because Zorlak needs your help." Kay jumped in.

"Great, now I'm taking orders from an imaginary Dream keeper. What does he need me to do? I can't do much from here, can I?" Drew questioned.

"He wants you to help the Nightmare Fairies to distract Dr. Cain and Dr. Borja so they don't figure out too much before we can complete our task there." Kay responded

"I'm almost afraid to ask, but what is a Nightmare Fairy?" Drew looked at her with wide eyes.

"They are the fairies that keep playing with Dr. Cain. One minute they have him thinking he has found the solution to get his new cognitive dream viewer working. Then just as he goes to write the program, they make him focus on another aspect of his research. They keep him on the verge of discovery with little mind games." Kay finished, out of breath.

"Are they messing with my head too?" Drew was getting more nervous by the moment. He couldn't even fathom what a nightmare fairy was or did and he didn't really want to.

"A Nightmare Fairy is one of the residents of Dreamland. They were sent there to assist Zorlak with their precognitive and telepathic powers. They can get into people's heads and see their thoughts and dreams and they can change the order of things to confuse people. They can also make people believe they are something they are not. Like Dr. Cain, for example, they are making him think he can actually see people's dreams against their will. What he doesn't realize is that even if he gets the remote viewing program to work, he will not see images unless the dreamer is semi-conscious and in total agreement to enable viewing." Kay was exhausted herself now.

"So, what exactly am I supposed to do?" Drew asked nervously.

"Keep him focused on as much misinformation as you can possibly think of. Like, tell him Tara can move things with her mind. That way he will refocus on telekinetic power and leave telepathic power alone for a day or so. That's all we need now to complete our task." Kay finished with a yawn.

"It looks like one dreamer is ready for an eventful journey now. Would you like to go to bed now, Sweetie?" Drew asked lovingly.

"As a matter of fact, I would. I am suddenly quite tired and even a little sleepy." Kay replied as she stood to leave the room.

"I will come in with you and tuck you in. I think I am going to reorganize some of my notes to keep ahead of all of this. I'll be in shortly to join you. I need to plan my strategy for whenever we see Dr. Cain again." Drew responded as he gently took Kay's arm and led the way to their room.

Kay's head barely hit the pillow and she was gone to Dreamland. Drew gently closed the door and returned to the study so he could reread his notes and actually plan some misinformation to impart to the good doctor, if he ever came back down from the attic, that is.

Drew was being aided by several of the Nightmare Fairies that had taken a liking to Tara and Kay and figured Drew could use a hand. When Drew finally drifted off, in his chair, they took him to an outer area in Dreamland for non-believers where they could gently show him the necessity of his family's involvement. Zorlak sensed their desire to assist and laughed. He may actually turn them into Dream Fairies after all.

Knowing Drew was safe in the hands of the fairies Zorlak turned his attention to Kays arrival, so they could begin the final phase of his plan to save it all.

Zorlak met Kay first to tell her that Drew was safe even though he was with the Nightmare Fairies, but he assured her that they were taking him to show him enough so he would be more comfortable.

"But aren't they going to play with his head and confuse him?" Kay said with a touch of concern in her voice.

"No, Kay, I told them they can only play with Dr. Cain and Dr. Borja, when he gets here." Zorlak responded as he led her down a hall to meet the others.

Chapter 23

Dr. Cain had retreated to his attic hide away. It had been painfully obvious that Drew was not yet ready to talk about this new idea of Dr. Cain's.

He had walked in on him this morning in the study and tried to convince him of the benefits of his new partnership and advise him of Dr. Borja's impending arrival. He was not a happy man. Dr. Cain only then realized that he must have awakened Drew. Dr. Cain also knew that he had been too hasty in his campaign to have Dr. Borja and his team accepted by the Prescott family. He should have waited for the others to arrive in the study before he launched into a full-scale campaign to have this new opportunity of theirs succeed.

Right now, Dr. Cain had to focus on the task at hand, this moment. Ruthie had always been trying to get him to do that. Live for the moment. Now, he had to focus because every moment counted, from here on in.

The first task was to recheck the family and property records for the new research team. He was now able to utilize the services of a full-time research team, and that is exactly what he intended to do. All of the boxes numbered and labeled were in the corner closest to the door. They would be easy for the new team to move them. They only had to go down the hallway into the east wing. This area had been sealed off for over thirty years earlier, when he and Ruthie bought the place. They had immediately gone about restoring this upper, east wing into the showplace it had been in its time.

This top level on the East side of the Manor was now as fully functional as a residence and also a laboratory but was still sealed off from the rest of the house.

There was over four thousand square feet of living space in this one level. In the city the same space would cost a fortune to lease of purchase and it was worth its space in gold to the Doctor and his new colleague. The history of Stone Cliff Manor itself was more than worth what he had paid for it years ago. The first thing they had done was starting to rebuild it to the original layout, complete with period furniture and accessories.

The next task to be completed was to organize all of the family histories that related directly to Tara and her family or to their ancestors. This was one of the most intriguing aspects of this family. Tara's great, great grandfather was a Civil War hero from Atlanta Georgia. The final battle he was in ended for him at the very site of the Sleep Centre Research & Diagnostic Psychic Facility, which was the new name for The Sleep Centre. Dr. Cain had changed it to The Sleep Centre from Stone Cliff Manor, which was its original name when he and Ruthie made it their home. Now Dr. Cain was changing its name once again to incorporate the areas of expertise that Dr. Borja was bringing to the partnership. He would call it The Institute for Sleep Research and Psychic Phenomenon Diagnostics. Dr. Cain had somehow always known that there was a more substantial and deeper connection between this property and Tara's family. The old Stone Cliff Manor had come a long way since the Civil War, and he was not about to let the historical events there cease.

Dr. Cain knew that there was a much deeper more substantial connection between this old Manor and Tara's family history. There were far too many coincidences that connected the family with this house, even in Tara's dreams there were connections to it. Anyone who had ever known Dr. Cain knew that he did not and would not ever believe in coincidence. He was a staunch believer in scientific cause and effect.

That everything that happened did so for a reason. He also believed that we may not always be privy to the reasons, but they do, nevertheless exist.

Dr. Cain was now starting to wonder about the existence of this entire psychic phenomenon he had read about. He pondered its validity and decided that if it would further his own research then he would give Dr. Borja a fair chance to convince him of their merit.

Dr. Cain labeled and stacked the last file box of family and property histories, where they intersected throughout several hundred years.

As he reached up to place the last box, of related Prescott family history, on top of the property research cartons, he stopped to consider, only for a moment, that he might be remembered as one of the most insightful and influential Scientists of his time. It may not be too late after all. Thinking about all of this intersecting family and property history, Dr. Cain was curious enough to begin his own research of the unexplained.

He was now curious enough to go online and search out related psychic phenomenon and, more specifically, psychic dreaming. Maybe he could unearth the theory or experiment that would solve the glitch in his current theory he was developing currently to remote view someone's dreams. He was starting to believe in unexplained phenomenon. He felt it too, had potential to be exploited scientifically.

After several hours of searching various theories Dr. Cain had narrowed it down to three that he would try with his videotapes of Tara dreaming.

No one else knew that he had been secretly taping all of Tara's dreams since she had arrived.

He had also run some tapes on Kay but with not as much success as with Tara. He thought this may be due to Kay's age or because she appeared to resist all contact or communication regarding Dreamland. He had electrodes sewn into the feather beds they slept on, and he had adjusted the temperature inside them for optimal conductivity.

These electrodes picked up the vibrations of the nerve endings in their skin as they slept. It could record all body temperature, brain activity, heart and breathing rates as well as the rapid eye movement phase of deep sleep that enables the brain to dream. Dr. Cain had always felt that brain waves should be as easy to replicate, decode and view as any other type of wave. After all, wasn't a brain wave similar to a microwave or a tidal wave?

They all have their similarities in that they all carry with them the strength of thousands of individual waves collected together. If he could decipher the code that had been used by nature to set up the molecules of the actual brain wave, then he could dissect it and recreate one to do further testing on. So, he had been collecting the brain waves of his patients for years.

This was the part of his old research that became so controversial that it ended not only his career but also the careers of anyone who had been foolish enough to have faith in him. He knew that the Beauregarde family had been infamous for their eccentricities and mental illnesses that ran through the whole bloodline for centuries.

Every generation had at least one all out crazy Beauregarde, but usually two or more. Maybe they were just ahead of their time.

If they had been psychic rather than crazy, then maybe Dr. Cain could unravel the Beauregarde mental illness mystery that had plagued their good names for too many years already. Dr. Cain wanted so badly to discover something that the Nightmare Fairies had a ball.

They had Dr. Cain fluctuating between thinking he could actually connect to Tara and follow her in her dreams to thinking that the Manor itself held the power of the ages and therefore all the necessary answers. He was maniacal about this research now and he could feel himself slipping away again. He exerted every bit of will he had left and fended off his impending break from reality. Ruthie had warned him not to get too close to physical and mental exhaustion, because that was the state he had been in just before his entire career and almost life began to unravel. He was barely able to close the attic office door behind him, he felt so weak.

He sat in a hallway chair that had been part of Ruthie's 'little touches' she had added in the form of decor around the sealed off wing. Dr. Cain laughed silently remembering how he had teased her about this very chair. He had thought it wasteful and ridiculous to have a chair so close to the office door, but as always, she had been right. Had that chair not been there Dr. Cain knew he would have fallen to the floor.

Dr. Cain struggled to catch his breath as he sat limply in the chair. His heart rate began to slow and his breath easier the longer he sat. He drifted off to sleep for a few moments and dreamt that Tara and her family were leaving in two days.

He awoke with such a jolt at the idea of them leaving, even in a dream that he almost fell out of his chair. He scurried to his feet and smoothed his hair down and then glanced at his watch.

He almost stumbled when he realized it was now almost Sunday evening. Where had the time gone, he wondered as he headed down the secret stairway to his own room? Once inside he showered, shaved and changed into clean clothes, then he was ready to make his appearance.

He was getting more curious by the hour and could hardly wait to speak to Dr. Borja face to face about all of their individual theories.

Chapter 24

Lutharious knew something was happening. He had been able to feel the presence of another one of Earth's protégées. He was getting tired of Zorlak and his interference with all of his plans to rule Dreamland and the Earth. It was time to act, once and for all, and get the reigns of Dreamland firmly in his grasp. He would gather his minions and wage a full-scale battle against Zorlak and the Chosen One. He could win this time, he had to, and he had promised himself that the next time he would make sure he could win before he even began.

Lutharious called together all the slimy ones in Dreamland that he depended upon, to bring him information about all of the events on Earth and in Dreamland. They took shape in many forms of creatures large and small, with and without legs and could easily blend in with any type of surroundings. Lutharious commanded them all to come and listen to him while he enlisted their support for his plan. Lutharious was even surprised at the sheer number of participants before him as he scanned the room for familiar faces.

"Now is the time to act! Swiftly, before they gain the force of the Bead. They are planning to repair the weakness in the fabric that separates us from Freedom. We cannot allow this to occur, or we will all perish! Band together now and help us save our homes!" Lutharious boomed from the centre podium.

There just happened to be a Throg in hiding behind one of the great walls of the coliseum when Lutharious was making his speech.

The minute Lutharious finished his speech and outlining his plan for the attack on Zorlak, and the three chosen helpers sent to save Dreamland, he was gone. The poor little Throg had been accidentally left behind on the last pass by the coliseum for the night. He knew his way home but had gotten distracted by the throngs of creatures heading for the great hall for Lutharious's speech. He had followed them, undetected and heard everything that Lutharious was planning.

At breakneck speed, the little Throg headed back to Zenithia and to Zorlak. The little Throg came in at a dead run and slid as he tried to stop. He managed to slide to a stop just short of banging into Zorlak.

"So, you were lost, weren't you?" Zorlak boomed at the Throg before him.

"No Sir, Zorlak, Sir, I got separated from my group when they made their last pass by the coliseum for the night." He took a ragged breath and continued.

"I heard Lutharious tell a group of hundreds that you, Zorlak, are going to destroy Dreamland if they all don't get together and defeat you and the 'little one', Sir." The Throg was exhausted but satisfied he had given Zorlak such important information.

Zorlak was very pleased with this new information because now he knew he had been right about Lutharious and his evil intentions. Zorlak retired to his private quarters so he could ponder this new information and adjust his strategy where necessary.

He knew he would have to get near someone or something that Lutharious trusted. He needed to get the message to him that Zorlak and Tara were trying to save Dreamland, and not destroy it. Deep down Zorlak knew that it would probably not make any difference to Lutharious. He knew Lutharious wanted to rule the Earth and Dreamland and thought his strategy would prevail. What he didn't realize was that any other plan than Zorlak's would mean the end of Earth and Dreamland forever. Zorlak was not trying to save himself; he was trying to save the world his co habitants needed for their survival. Zorlak also figured that Lutharious was deliberately lying to the masses to gain their support. Lutharious would do anything to help himself, even if it hurt Dreamland and Earth and Zorlak knew it.

Zorlak revisited the route he had intended that they take this evening to retrieve the Bead of Light. He had selected the path of least resistance; at least that was what he thought he was doing. He now had to watch out for certain areas where there might be evil followers of Lutharious hiding in the dark shadows.

While he pondered the very best route to the weakened area Zorlak led Kay to where Tara and Elizabeth were waiting. They joined hands again and began floating around the foggy corners of the inner core passageway leading them closer to the area that held the secrets of Dreamland. The internal lining of Dreamland that had the weakness was deeply hidden within the folds of time.

It could not be seen with the naked eye unless you are Tara with her gift of acute vision. She had no problems navigating the way to the location that Zorlak had described to her in detail.

Tara had to be able to recognize it and she felt she already knew how. She felt that if she touched the affected area, she would feel the very weakness and instinctively know how to heal it and save everyone. She could feel her own increase in inner strength and was reassured. She knew that the fate of her family and her entire planet rested squarely in the palm of her hands, and she was somewhat overwhelmed.

Zorlak kept repeating the route to the Bead of Light like it would be an easier journey the more he spoke the words. Tara could not help daydreaming about the route herself. She was looking forward to the upcoming challenge of this evening. They were actually going to go and get the Bead of Light. In her mind's eye, Tara had already seen their journey and she was confident she could accomplish this first crucial task. Kay and Elizabeth listened to Zorlak intently as if they were trying to wring out some hidden meaning in Zorlak's words. Tara had enough of this delay, and she wanted to go for the trial run Zorlak had been promising her.

Finally, Tara's impatience paid off and Zorlak was finished his lecture and they were actually ready to go. As they grasped hands once again and felt the surge of life power that surged within them, they began to float. As the energy intensified, they floated higher until Zorlak could no longer see them.

He sighed, heavily and returned to his private quarters to relax and deal with all the other possible loose ends that could destroy the fragile plan they had to save both worlds.

Zorlak needed to get in touch with those little Nightmare Fairies and set them straight and he needed a distraction so he wouldn't worry. The Nightmare Fairies were a good place to start because then he could gather a little information on Dr. Cain and Drew and everything else there. This was a major loose end, especially when there were so many different angles to consider.

Whenever Zorlak thought about the magnitude of this tragedy. This had been the very worst of any so far in the history of Dreamland and Earth. Zorlak knew all about the history and the connections between Tara, her family, the Sleep Centre and Dreamland and he could not risk Dr. Cain and Dr. Borja stumbling onto it. That would be a disaster and none of the residents of either world could afford to take the chance.

Drew could not get too close either as he too had connections to the Sleep Centre and Dreamland. These were from his own family's history and went back generations.

The sleep doctors could speculate all they wanted but they would never be able to obtain any concrete evidence of this parallel universe that is Dreamland. Without this evidence and eyewitness testimonials Dr. Cain and Dr. Borja would never gain the credibility they would require to ever obtain the research grants that would be necessary to complete a full, provable and credible research study. Neither of these professional researchers had very good reputations. Both had been asked to step down from prestigious, powerful scientific organizations and were black balled by the entire scientific community.

Chapter 25

As soon as Kay and Elizabeth joined their hands with Tara, they could feel it. They had absolutely no idea what they felt but they knew tonight would be full of surprises for all of them. The three bobbed around corners and swerved around curves as Tara led them blindly into the area she sought. When they finally landed, there they were back in front of the Bejeweled Doors; only they were smaller than the other ones in the cavernous hall. The doors swung open silently and rested gently on the opposite wall. Tara floated slightly ahead of her mother and grandmother so she could see what was in store for them first. All she saw was Zorlak, sitting with his chin in his large claw like hand resting his elbow on top of his bent knee. It was obvious he was concerned as well as deep in thought. Tara floated closer so she could whisper and be heard by only him.

"Zorlak, I am here now, all is well, and we will prevail." Tara whispered softly into the air.

"My Little One, you are back, and just in time. There is much to be done. I need to show you where we need to go to obtain the Bead of Light with the power of the ages. This will assist us in saving Earth and Dreamland because it is the only known source of power left that can truly overcome evil in its purest form. Lutharious has obtained more power. He has increased his following by lying about our intentions. He has spread the rumor that we are trying to destroy it all rather than let Lutharious rule over it all." Zorlak finally took a deep breath and continued, "Now, I am having the Throgs locate a trusted one close to Lutharious so that we can send word of our true intentions. We will send it to whoever is the closest to him so at least one more in Dreamland would know the truth. I must accompany you now no matter what the risk."

"The more that find out the real truth the better, as this will strengthen our power. We represent the good in all of man and creature kind. Lutharious and his band of rebels are the clear representation of pure evil. Unfortunately, we are not permitted to force the truth on anyone as Lutharious forces lies on the weak ones that follow him. We must be patient with those that seek the truth to find it. That is why we follow God; we know he represents ultimate good in all." Zorlak stood now and led the ways to the anteroom and the chamber beyond.

Here he would impart the final changes to the directions and instructions to follow in order to find the Bead of Light hidden deep in the Underground Chamber called Belanger. No one knew why but some thought it was one of the ancients' names from back at the beginning. Some even said it was a human that helped get it all started and it was his or her name. I do not remember which. Everyone just knew that no one was ever allowed to go in there without direct permission form Zorlak and the Directors of the Law.

The Directors of the Law were an ancient panel of old souls sitting in the background taking notes and transcribing history in the making. The transcribers work tirelessly as there are so many willing volunteers, they may not get another opportunity for a long while. They work for days until the panel takes a rest and then they rest too. They had given Zorlak permission to take Tara, Kay and Elizabeth into the forbidden temple and the chamber, which held the Bead of Light. Tara had to see this gem in order to gather sufficient power to save both dynasties. Now, Zorlak must lead these humans through the dungeons of Dreamland into the underbelly where the parents of the Nightmare Fairies lived.

It was indeed the scariest part of Dreamland Tara had ever seen. She still was not afraid, and she couldn't understand why not. Tara just shrugged it off and figured it was because Zorlak was with her, and she could also feel God within her guiding her through. She had never really been scared in Dreamland only comfortable. Tara felt like she was invincible whenever she was in Dreamland. After all, she could fly, walk through walls, and soar around within the walls with the Squigglies like embers in the fire. No wonder she felt like she could do anything, she probably could. Tara was excited about being one of the few humans that had ever been allowed within these walls, let alone on our way to the Chamber. She could hardly wait to get there.

Kay was not so sure any of this was a good idea, but it didn't seem like she really had much of a choice, so she just silently went along for the ride and to lend support whenever and wherever necessary. Elizabeth was in the same boat, she was just going with the flow and hoping Zorlak knew what he was doing.

As all three glided silently through twists and turns in the inner walls and halls of the underground of Dreamland each new level smelled worse than the one before it and it got darker and colder as they made their decent. Suddenly, Zorlak stopped short, Tara and her family almost crashed into him. There in front of them was Lutharious and a few of his hoodlums, blocking their path.

"Well, aren't these beautiful ladies you are in the company of, my old friend? Please introduce me to these humans of yours, Zorlak." Lutharious said while leering at Kay and Tara. When his eyes met Elizabeth's gaze he froze, on the spot. "Well, Grandmother of us all, please forgive me, I was unaware of your personal involvement in this disaster." Lutharious said to Elizabeth as he bowed his head slightly.

"Lutharious." Zorlak's voice boomed out above all other noises.

"Sit down and listen to me, now! Before it is too late, and you have killed us all." Zorlak finished in a hiss.

"I am not the evil one, Zorlak, that is you and you have known this all along but yet, you call me evil. I am the Savior of Dreamland and not a human child and her female family members. Surely, you know you need a real army to win in a battle with our warriors. We have trained all of our lives for this very moment. There is a weakness in Dreamland, and I will find it so I can strengthen it myself and then use it to my advantage. I will gain the power necessary to strengthen the weakness in Dreamland." Lutharious was ranting now.

"I am the only one that will be able to gain the power within the bead of light. The Directors, God, Zorlak and my family have chosen me. It is out of our hands now. We must follow our destiny." Tara was stating these words as if by rote. It sounded like a well-prepared speech to be given to a crowd of unbelievers. She knew Lutharious was not going to like what she was saying but she was saying it anyway.

"Girl!" Lutharious bellowed.

"Do not speak to me in that tone." Tara spat and glared him in the eye.

Lutharious said very little during the balance of that entire confrontation between Zorlak and Lutharious's followers. Lutharious just stood back and glared at Tara from a distance. His rage was barely hidden. He had never been so blatantly insulted in front of his own followers. Zorlak was explaining that they had been lied to and that he was trying to save both worlds. Tara and her family had been selected to assist in saving both worlds. This was a real crisis this time, not just a drill. Lutharious was losing support the longer Zorlak spoke.

By the time Zorlak had finished all he had to say there was only a handful of supporters left beside Lutharious.

Within moments Lutharious was gone, in a flurry of wings and grunts. Tara looked at Zorlak and simple stated, "Shall we move on now?" and continued on their way down to the underside. It stunk but it was a safe haven to slip into the inner sanctum from, although it was messy. As soon as they had all passed through and into the inner sanctum where the Bead of Light was stored, they were instantly clean again and all dressed in white, even Zorlak, which was a weird sight, him being completely jet black. The Squigglies in the outer walls had tormented Lutharious and his followers by guiding them down dead end passes and into dark caverns all the way back to the meeting hall. Lutharious was not impressed by this evening's goings on. Something had to be done about that kid and her female family members. They would ruin everything he had worked his whole life for, control of Dreamland and the end of him answering to Zorlak. Lutharious headed back to his own small cavern to plot and scheme a way to get the kid and her family to go away. They were humans so they were afraid of something. He would send in the Nightmare Fairies with the experience, not the nice ones that were playing with Dr. Cain but the real nightmare ones. The kind of nightmares that you think are real and you wake up bathed in sweat and shaking while you pray to God to give you strength to get through it all.

Now, they could refocus on the destiny for this evening's journey, getting the Bead of Light. They gingerly picked their way through the next level of vegetation as they wound closer to the Underground Chamber called Belanger. Within a few short minutes they were nearing the entrance to the hidden cavern.

Zorlak led them through the small opening in the wall and into the inner room. They gradually made their way into the room and could not believe their eyes.

Tara saw it first and she slowed down considerably until she came to a full stop and her little mouth dropped open. There in front of her was the most beautiful sight she had even seen. The Bead of Light rested gently between two platinum claws, suspended in midair, within a sphere of crystal and safely encased in the inner vault. The Bead of Light was glowing in various shades of purples, pinks, greens and blues. Tara didn't even realize that only she and Zorlak were able see it through the solid granite rock wall. It shone brighter than Zorlak had ever seen it.

They all heard the humming sound and Tara just glided closer to the sound. When she got really close it was a deeper note, but still a humming noise. Tara floated through a hidden doorway that had just appeared for her and knelt down in front of a huge oval container. Inside it were the platinum claws that were suspended on either side of it. It was a solid crystal football shaped sphere with lights pulsating out from inside of it. Tara got even closer, and Kay's throat started to constrict as she took in a breath to scream, she realized it was too late, now her daughter had each of her hands on either side of the sphere and the glow was crawling up Tara's arms.

Suddenly, as they all looked on, dumbfounded, Tara's entire body began to glow, and the bead evaporated into her as quickly as they could blink twice it was all over and the bead was gone. Everyone was exhausted and Tara really looked like she may need medical attention.

They flew silently back through their previous path as quickly as they could and returned to just inside the small Bejeweled Doors.

"I really think that Tara should see a doctor. Mother, what do you think?" Kay asked pleadingly.

"I shall keep her here tonight, all night. When you awaken in the morning Tara will not. Keep everything and everyone away from her until noon on Earth and she will be just fine." Zorlak said with a wave of his huge hand and the next thing Kay knew, she was back in her bed and awake to the bright Sunday morning sun.

"We can't wake Tara up until noon, Drew." Kay whispered into her husband's ear. "I locked her door and only I have the key." She finished as she gently kissed his ear.

"Great!" Drew whispered back as he grabbed her back into bed and convinced her to go back to sleep for another hour or so, Tara was sleeping anyway.

Chapter 26

Fresh from their battle with Lutharious and Tara having the Bead of Light enter into her being. Kay was a bit weary as she headed for the study to see if Drew was there yet. She knew she would soon have to go wake up Tara, but Kay wanted to give Zorlak as much time as he needed to help make Tara feel better than she had last night. Kay knew that Elizabeth was not going to leave Tara's side the entire time she stayed there. Kay had nothing to worry about. That didn't stop her it only slowed her down a little. Now all she worried about was how her unsuspecting husband was dealing with all of this nonsense. As Kay entered the study, she was struck with a feeling of Deja vu. She felt that this moment had happened before, as she looked at Drew sound asleep in his chair with his book on his chest and his glasses about to fall off of his nose. She gently took off his glasses and covered him over with a quilt. She then set out for Tara's room. When she reached the top of the stairs, she saw the now familiar red glow coming from under her bedroom door. This time Kay did not panic. She calmly reached for the knob and as she got closer, she could feel the unbearable heat emanating from the handle. She jumped back and waited for the glow to subside and then she left to go lie down again. She was totally exhausted and Zorlak had already told her the red glow keeps Tara from being awakened while she is in a vulnerable state in Dreamland. It is on Earth protection from Dreamland.

Zorlak had said that the relationship between the humans and the creatures was because of a loving little girl from centuries ago that would not let her dreams die. She helped to forge the sometimes-spirited truce between the creature world and the human world.

There was at least one evil force at work in Dreamland and that was because of Lutharious and his poisonous words and dreadful deeds.

But was there a separate evil force working with Lutharious from outside of Dreamland?

Zorlak decided he would look into this Dr. Cain to see if he was a human or a creature and whether or not he could be trusted. He needed to contact the Nightmare Fairies and see what they had been able to learn about the "good doctor" and his crazy ideas. He must summon them to him so he could question them.

Kay just wanted a relaxing Sunday by the fire and maybe a stroll out to the trails and have a picnic, but Tara was intent on her parents hearing her feelings and experiences from her dream the night before. She was all wound up and ready to share. She nattered on and on for over an hour. Drew was getting tired from typing and Kay needed a nap. She was still exhausted and really wanted to lie down for a little while. Kay rose to her feet and stretched while Drew was stretching out his fingers and his arms.

"I'm going to go and lie down for a little while; I think I need some more rest for tonight." Kay said over her shoulder on her way out of the room.

"Good night, I mean good nap, Mommy." Tara giggled at her mother as she blew her a kiss and left.

"I'll be in to tuck you in shortly, Kay." Drew said to Kay as she left the room.

"Now that Mommy is gone, I need to talk to you alone Daddy." Tara sputtered excitedly.

"What is it you don't want your mother to know about, Tara?" Drew questioned.

"Nothing bad, Daddy." Tara giggled again.

"I just want to explain about Dreamland and not have Mommy hear it all again." Tara continued, undeterred.

"Well, Zorlak has a plan to get me into the inner lining of Dreamland so that I can locate the exact position of the weakness in the fabric of time that separates us from Dreamland." Tara was very serious in her detailed explanation, so Drew made sure he was taking notes.

He could always decipher his own shorthand later when both of his girls slept. He had not been able to sleep very much since he had arrived at the Sleep Centre. Drew found it ironic that he was unable to sleep at a diagnostic Sleep Centre that specialized in sleep disorders. The funny thing was that the sleep expert, Dr. Cain hadn't even noticed yet.

"So, tonight we are going to the inner city of Dreamland. It's called Zenithia and it is beautiful, all in white and silver with that icicle like things hanging from the ceiling. You know what I mean Daddy, the same as in those caves we went to last year." Tara insisted. "That is how I get through to the inside where I can find the weakness. It is in the fabric of time, but I think it looks like a sheet. It is what keeps us apart and that, according to Zorlak, is a good thing. Tara finally stopped to catch her breath."

Drew jumped in quickly to give her a chance to catch her breath and relax for a minute or two. "Honey, relax now and just breathe. I know what they're called; stalactites and they're made of centuries of dripping sand over each other and the rocks the hang from."

"Then the water continues to run down it for centuries more after we are long gone, leaving more layers of solidified sand and gravel. It's like natures cement. They are beautiful and only naturally pure in the deepest caverns in the world. There are very few of those left, unexplored." Drew rambled on and on. He was wondering if he should suggest a nap when Kay reappeared in the doorway and suggested a walk through the paths all over the grounds and maybe even have a picnic in the woods.

Tara jumped to her feet and ran from the room screaming behind her "I'm going to change. I'll be right back." and she was gone.

"What is going on, Kay?" Drew asked, "I thought you were asleep. Why are you up already?" Drew finished as he held her in his arms and hugged her close to him.

Kay just shrugged and said "I feel like getting some fresh air and exercise today. It is a beautiful day, especially on these grounds." Kay finished with a grin." Besides, I want to play hooky today and not even think about where we are or why we're here. Just be together and have some fun." Kay was determined. She had already gotten the cooks to help her get a picnic together. It was spectacular and it was well worth taking a small wagon, to carry it all in, behind them throughout their walk.

The air was fresh and clean with the scent of flowering shrubs in the warm breeze. It felt like Heaven, and they all just soaked it up. There was very little in the way of conversation for the rest of the afternoon as they were all lost in their own thoughts and plans for the evening hours.

The rest of Sunday passed very peacefully at the Sleep Centre, and they all gathered in the kitchen at dinnertime, cleaned, dressed and hungry.

The first time anyone had seen Dr. Cain in a day and a half. Kay and Drew were starting to get restless with the lack of progress they were seeing in this environment. They decided this would be a good time to discuss it with their daughters Doctor, the fact that she was doing no better here than she had at home. They felt she should be sent back home and any further treatment could be done on an outpatient basis. Drew and Kay both knew that this would be the perfect way to help derail Dr. Cain's progress in the area of viewing Tara's dreams.

Drew would see to it that the doctor was being watched from this point onward until his family left this place, for good. Dr. Cain was intent on convincing Drew and Kay that Dr. Borja's arrival would speed up the process of evaluating the ability Tara had to dream things into reality. Tara actually "thought" her Father to visit the Sleep Centre.

Tara was fed and cozied up in front of the fireplace on her mat with her blanket and pillow. She was lying there silently thinking about her evening ahead in Dreamland. She was storing up her energy just in case she needed it later. She was following all of the instructions Zorlak had given her.

They had eaten in the kitchen in silence and followed each other into the study with coffee for the adults and hot chocolate for Tara. The huge overstuffed antique chairs were ample for the three of them to sit and all enjoy the fire. It was the perfect arrangement for a quiet conversation among people passionate about varying viewpoints.

Kay decided she should start the ball rolling "So, Dr. Cain are you ever even going to examine Tara?" sounding a little more hostile than she had wanted to.

"Are we making any progress at all, with you hidden in your attic all of the time. Now, I hear you want to bring in another Doctor to speed things up. For whom? We haven't seen any results whatsoever." Kay was almost panting when she finished.

"I think that what my wife is saying is that although this is a beautiful spot for a vacation this is not supposed to be one." Drew explained as calmly as he could. "I really think we all need a good night's sleep and then we can reconvene on all topics at breakfast, first thing in the morning." Drew finished as he drained his coffee mug and stood up. Kay stood then and Tara popped up. Dr. Cain had no choice but to stand as well, so he too, stood. They exchanged pleasant, albeit strained good night's and all headed for their respective bedrooms for the night.

Drew and Kay both tucked Tara in so they could tell her together how much they loved her. They closed her door and grasped hands as they walked down the hall and stairs into their own room. They snuggled up and Kay was asleep almost immediately. Drew held her close to him as she shuddered as if she were freezing. Finally, Kay settled down and she and Drew drifted off for a precious few hours of sleep.

Dr. Cain went to his study relieved that he avoided answering any of the Prescott's questions, but he knew it would all have to come out in the morning. He had to rush tonight to get enough information ready for them as he could based on his research to date. He was trying to find a way to discuss it without having to bring up his dream video program. He wanted to be truthful but not divulge what Tara as a test subject really meant to him and his continued research.

Chapter 27

They found Zorlak pacing back and forth in front of the bejeweled inner doors again. His hand rubbing up and down slowly over his chin. Zorlak had plotted their entire course and Tara had committed it to memory. The three managed to find their way quickly and quietly up to the Doors, the Bejeweled Inner Doors. They had flown a course of amazing speed. Tara took each corner like she was in a race and Elizabeth and Kay were concerned for their safety more than once along the way. Tara had passed her last test and was able to make the journey to the core of Dreamland, alone. The three of them would go together as far as the opening to the core and there, Kay and Elizabeth would remain until Tara returned from her journey into the core and back. By then the power should be dispersing to the areas of Dreamland and all would be well.

She had taken a number of the shortcuts that Zorlak had insisted they take. Tara had no idea why but, she followed it anyway, after all she was only 7 years old. She was the ultimate "little one". She knew that there was no good way to get there but Zorlak had plotted the route of least resistance and she knew she was ready now.

That had been the big plan all along. Tara had always suspected there was a new kind of energy she had with her mother and grandmother, but she only recently learned how critical it was for the survival of all she knew. She, like usual, had to be the strong one, the strongest link, the glue that held the two worlds so near and also far away.

Now it was time to finally test Tara's ability to conquer evil and save the day. Some were very skeptical and maybe still are, but there are her fans, the believers. Her Dreamland connection was threefold stronger than any other active Dreamland visitor.

Her mother and grandmother could go to Dreamland at will and apparently had always possessed this very power. That alone helped to make Tara the savior; it was her youth and pure insight into the hearts and minds of the purest evil that exists anywhere.

She had vanished into thin air and into the great wall, on numerous occasions, now here she was determined to save a world she was supposed to know nothing about. Her young age had concerned both Kay and Elizabeth, but Tara pressed on. The Sleep Centre had become a cat and mouse game between the nightmare fairies and Dreamland visits. Poor Drew had just gone with the flow of things and was always there in the morning to hug them both.

Tara had learned very quickly how to navigate around Dreamland, undetected. She had really enjoyed that part, especially when she went to see Seth. They would play and he would brag about his work with the "Little Ones". Then Tara was off to learn some more. It went by in a blink for Kay and Elizabeth, and they were not even aware that she was gone. Tara had learned awake and asleep, in her dreams and in their notes. Tara met her parents in the big kitchen every morning for breakfast. After that they would compare notes and write down new experiences in their now quite thick notebook. Her father was busy typing it over for her.

The main lesson Tara had learned throughout all of this was that family stays together and always supports its members no matter what the threat.

There is always safety in numbers and what better group to be in than your own family. Tara was seeing parallel worlds both guided by the same God she had already learned about in Church. It was really cool to be this close to things she had only heard about before.

The one who is evil enough to destroy everything sacred to himself in order to make the opposite party lose? That is not the mark of a hero but a mark of a coward. Lutharious must be the worst type of coward as he sends innocents to carry his words and deeds through to fruition. He had not yet showed up for any of the meetings Tara had requested in her time here. Now, it would be too late as the three women had to defeat Lutharious and his kind in order to protect the existence of both worlds.

This was a recurring dream of Tara's for a long time now, this particular journey into the heart of Dreamland. Tara was filled with an almost overwhelming sense of purpose, freedom and life. She knew instinctively that their life would never be the same again.

Tara knew that this was the ultimate opportunity for her and maybe even in her lifetime. She knew that she was ready for whatever Zorlak and Lutharious had in mind for her.

Everything was about to change drastically and permanently, never to return to life, as they had known it. As Tara scanned her memory, she felt secure in the knowledge that her father was safe in his chair in the study, sound asleep, no doubt. Dr. Cain if he was asleep then the Nightmare Fairies were having their fun. If not, then he was probably in his research lab in the attic cooking up some crazy new strategy to get at Tara's dreams.

Kay felt the cold surrounding her as they floated, but she was not cold. There seemed to be a glow emanating from the three of them and a kind of misty fog encompassing them as they floated further into the underbelly of Dreamland.

There was a maze of evil that would have to be beaten and this would be more than a little bit difficult. Her, she was just a little girl and she was going to save the world. Tara could not believe her luck. She was the one picked to save Dreamland and the Earth. "Cool, isn't it?" she whispered to herself as they settled in front of the huge doors. Right on the other side of these doors was the beginning of the evil maze that had to be navigated prior to any success within the inner walls. Tara took in a deep breath as she tried to prepare herself, mentally for whatever was on the other side of these doors.

The new beginning or the bitter end lay just around the next twist in the tunnel. The spot where the ultimate showdown took place, and all hell was bound to break loose.

As the way got narrower and the light dimmed, Kay and Elizabeth had more difficulty navigating through it. Tara held their hands tightly and guided them around sharp turns and down dingy hallways by the dozens.

They were heading to the Amethyst Door that would lead them out of the safest regions of Dreamland and into what was commonly called the 'underbelly' and Zorlak could not accompany them.

They were very close now and slowed down considerably as there was a huge gathering in front of the doors. Tara was a little concerned, but Zorlak had warned her to be ready for anything.

Tara had to strengthen the outer layer of protective fabric from the inside. This was because, although Zorlak had pinpointed the exact location, there was no safe way to determine in which layer of the protective fabric the actual weakest part was.

They knew it was dangerously close to the outermost layer. This was the most vulnerable because it was on the outside against the Earth's protective fabric. If, by some long shot, there was an identical weakness in the outermost layer of Earth that matched up with the same weakness in that layer of Dreamland. That would spell immediate disaster as both worlds would collapse into each other and no one would survive, from either world. The chances were only one in a billion, but Tara was aware of it, as a possibility only. She and Zorlak had spoken at length about possible ways to heal the weakness. Tara was all for her going inside the protective fabric folds to locate the weakness. Tara also believed that she could heal it with her touch. The only real problem with that strategy was that there might be a power surge when she touched it and there was no safe way to determine how much damage would be done if there were one. Tara and Zorlak finally rejected this idea because of the worst-case scenario would be that, unfortunately, was that the possibility would be greater of collapse if the resulting implosion were to cause the weakness to tear wide open. Then both worlds would explode out into space together, also, no survivors. They were looking for better odds.

The worried pair finally decided that the best place to strengthen was from the core out. Tara would take the spiral down as far as she could go and then do what she knew she should. This will create enough energy, pure energy to protect the outer layers from as deep into Dreamland as the very heart of it. They had planned for Tara to float and spiral back up again pouring her pure light over everything in its path.

The power would emanate all the way through Dreamland but in a safer way. The power would reduce in potency as it made its way all through each layer of the protective fabric of time and heal the weakness by providing another layer of protection throughout the inside.

Chapter 28

The real issue right now was the swelling crowd that Tara could see gathering in front of the Amethyst Door. Tara was shaken at the first sight of them and then she straightened her back, raised her chin and floated with her mother and grandmother to a spot just in front of the crowd. The three were practically pinned up against the Door and the crowd was coming closer. Starting from the very back there was a ripple through the mob and then Lutharious appeared in the middle of the mass of creatures. He stood up as straight as he could and towered over the rest of the crowd.

"You dare to defy the great Lutharious, Humans?" He bellowed.

"I have been chosen to repair the weakness in the protective fabric before it breaks through and destroys us all!" Tara bellowed back at him defiantly.

"I will stop you! You must not believe Zorlak. He wants to rule Dreamland and the Earth, and he has tricked you and your family. Follow me and I will show you what I mean." Lutharious said with a wave of his huge hand, and he turned and disappeared into the cavern next to the Amethyst Door.

"No one tells me who or what to believe, ever!" Tara spat at him.

"I will kill you and your family here and on Earth. My spies are there now, at your precious Sleep Centre and they are awaiting my instructions." Lutharious roared fiercely.

"I will carry out my destiny and you, Sir will obey!" Tara appeared to be losing her temper. Kay and Elizabeth had never seen this side of Tara before. They weren't sure if they liked this new Tara. She certainly looked and sounded all grown up now.

Tara's eyes blazed with a deepening red glow that unnerved her mother. The more people fear the more they are willing to tolerate. Tara needed Kay and Elizabeth for backup so there was no time for fear. They must stand firm and tall on Tara's behalf and lend her the power she would need from them in order to complete this crucial task. Tara could handle it with little or no fear, so Kay and Elizabeth just followed suit. The power of these three was the final ingredient required to save both worlds and Tara was the only being on either world that possessed all of them.

"You, Lutharious are forbidden to go any further on this path by decree of the Ancient's. I am here to enforce this decree if you make it necessary. I would appreciate obedience out of respect for my grandmother, Elizabeth, the Calming One. I am our future, and you are expendable. Either you are with us or against us. It is entirely your decision, but we need to know as soon as possible. Your decision Sir, now!" Tara finished in a raised tone of voice.

"I will obey you, child, but only out of respect for your grandmother. We will both follow Zorlak's instructions, as he is our leader. I will wait here with our army. We will be ready to take you prisoner if you fail to save us all. When you return you may be answering to me for a change." Lutharious gloated as he readied his troops for battle, just in case.

"I appreciate the respect you show for all of us, our families and our laws." Tara replied a little calmer, now.

"I will enter these doors ahead of you Mother and Grandmother. I will make sure it is safe and then come back for you. If I don't come back in two hours then wait exactly ten more minutes and then run like hell. Zorlak thinks that the entire spiral down and back is only three minutes total. No problem." Tara bragged, grinning.

Elizabeth spoke directly to her granddaughter for the first time since the last part of this journey began. "Tara, Dear I am so proud of you my little Angel. I knew I would still be around to see this day if I agreed to assist Dreamland after my death. You don't have to do it if you don't want to. There is no obligation to become a card- carrying member of anything. I wanted to stay in touch with you and now with your mother too. Thank you for giving me my daughter back. I love you, Angel" Elizabeth stopped and wiped a tear off her cheek. She knew this could be the last time any of them ever saw each other again, on any plane of existence.

Kay was next as she grabbed her daughter and hugged her too hard. "I'm sorry, Honey. I just can't imagine life without us together." Kay stammered.

"Mama, I love you forever and for always here or there, wherever we are. We don't really need a world in order to be close because we are all one and you don't get much closer than that." Tara finished with a giggle. "Mommy, I will be really careful and the Squigglies will be in the surface walls all the way down and back to light my way and watch for hidden threats." Tara explained.

"Honey, I know we need to help all we can. I understand and I am so proud of you." Kay repeated as she hugged Tara.

Tara turned to face the Amethyst Door and when she raised her right hand the door started to open, silently. Tara floated in through the opening and looked around briefly for enemies. Seeing none she floated back to get her mother and grandmother.

The three joined hands once again and floated in through the doorway. The minute they were safely inside the door slammed shut with such a bang they all jumped. Led by a child they continued on their journey, floating cautiously through the unknown.

Tara could feel the pure evil that surrounded them as they floated through the darkest and dirtiest caverns and tunnels you could imagine. They were silent in their descent into the underbelly. The Evil Maze was supposed to be under control or, so Lutharious had promised her. They should have no troubles on the way there. What Lutharious had neglected to tell Tara was the rest of what will happen to her and her family if she failed.

Tara could see the Squigglies in the inner walls guiding them and she could feel the Throgs inside the walls watching from behind and all sides. She could also feel the incredible glow inside of her from the Bead of Light and this gave her strength.

They reached the very edge of the spiral of doom. That is what Tara started calling it. She said it made her laugh and not be afraid. Kay and Elizabeth gave her one last hug as she stepped up onto the sides of the crater. Instead of a downward spiral, as she had expected, she was floating upwards hovering over a crystal globe. The higher Tara floated the brighter she glowed. Up in spirals and full extension of arms spinning her power out of her and into the core of Dreamland. Tara never even flinched at this new twist since there had already been so many. She was standing tall with her back arched and her hair hanging down her back, face pointing at the ceiling and her arms fully extended and out over her head. She was spinning and so was the globe, but the globe was rotating the opposite way from Tara. The power was pouring out of every part of her being as she spun around. The power coming out of her fingers was the strongest and easiest to actually aim of all of them.

Tara had been to the bottom and was halfway back when there was a huge bolt of light that went straight up through Tara and onward up and out of sight. A huge bang was also heard throughout the tunnels. Suddenly there was no light at all and only silence filled the cavern. When the light returned Tara was nowhere to be found. Kay and Elizabeth were frantic.

Zorlak explained to them that Tara had gone to the weakest point of the fabric of time and had actually made herself part of the wall, as only her presence could mend the weakness and make it strong again.

Zorlak assured them that Tara was safe and that he knew where she was. He advised Kay that Tara may not awaken on earth for a few weeks as the ending was performed, but not to be alarmed because she was being tended to continuously.

Chapter 29

Tara opened her eyes and blinked against the bright ceiling lights. She struggled to sit up and realized she had been strapped in. Now, she was starting to panic. Her eyes began to dart around the room and then she saw her. "Momma!" Tara shrieked, "We did it! We saved them all! Zorlak must be happy." Tara was talking a mile a minute.

Kay was not far from her daughters' side, nor had she been for the past several weeks. Tara had been unconscious ever since the last trip to Dreamland. Weeks had passed and Drew had gone back to the city. So much had happened and Tara had slept through it all. "Yes, my little Angel, you saved the day." Kay said soothingly.

"We can catch up over the next weeks while you get your strength back. I am just so glad to see you back, our little Angel." Kay whispered as she kissed Tara's forehead.

In the time it took Kay to stand back up straight Tara had drifted off to sleep this time, not the deep unconscious state she had been in. Kay could call Drew and let him know they would be ready to come home now as soon as he could get there to pick them up.

Kay sat next to her daughter's bed in the antique rocker and pondered all they had been through and how they would even feel normal again. She closed her eyes long enough to drift off into a dreamless, restful sleep for the first time in her life.

Drew was only too happy to take a few days off and come up to get his girls immediately. Now they could heal as a family and let the crazy Dream Doctors play around with all the research tapes and journals that they had managed to compile on Tara and her family.

While Tara and Kay waited for Drew to arrive, they quietly discussed the adventure they had in Dreamland, leading up to how they could not locate Tara and Zorlak had made sure she was well looked after during her time spent within the fabric. Tara hadn't even realized she had been out for so long nor had she even known what her body and mind were doing on their own.

Tara had a million questions about the bolt of light, the ensuing darkness and where, exactly she had been for all those weeks. During the next few days, it would all come back to Tara and as it did she could discuss it with her mother or grandmother.

As they left the yard of the Sleep Centre Tara couldn't help but think that she had not yet seen the last of it or Dr. Cain.

So, back at the Sleep Centre, things were heating up for Dr. Cain and Dr. Borja. Finally, alone in the dusty, smelly attic lab, they began to catalog all of their data onto two separate computer systems.

One was linked to their newest invention and the other linked to the research and recording centre. Dr. Cain had gotten away with telling the Prescott's very little about what research he had gathered on Tara or how he planned to use it in the coming months.

Both Doctors saw Tara as their ticket back from being blacklisted and shunned by their own colleagues. They felt that their groundbreaking discovery and techniques could change the way sleep was viewed all over the world. They would be famous and wildly successful and sought after for their opinions on everything from sleep disorders to viewing a patient's dreams on videotape.

This research would take the better part of 5 years to complete, and they were still working on the bugs out of their new video invention. Tara sensed they were up to no good, but for the time being she just wanted to try and be a normal little girl for a while. She still went to Dreamland whenever she could and she knew that sooner or later Dr. Cain's and Borja's paths would cross hers, but until then she was enjoying being 7 years old again.

www.ingramcontent.com/pod-product-compliance
Lightning Source LLC
LaVergne TN
LVHW091047100526
838202LV00077B/3064